BABY ISLAND

BABY ISLAND

by

CAROL RYRIE BRINK

Pictures by Helen Sewell

Aladdin Paperbacks

Aladdin Paperbacks
An imprint of Simon & Schuster Children's Publishing Division
1230 Avenue of the Americas, New York, NY 10020
Copyright © 1937 by The Macmillan Company
All rights reserved including the right of reproduction
in whole or in part in any form.
First Aladdin Paperbacks edition, 1993
Printed in the United States of America
25 24 23 22 21

Library of Congress Cataloging-in-Publication Data
Brink, Carol Ryrie, date.
Baby Island / by Carol Ryrie Brink; pictures by Helen Sewell. —
1st Aladdin Books ed.
p.   cm.
Summary: Twelve-year-old Mary Wallace and her ten-year-old sister Jean
survive the wreck of an ocean liner on its way to Australia and manage to
make it to a seemingly deserted island in a lifeboat with four babies.
ISBN-13: 978-0-689-71751-2   ISBN-10: 0-689-71751-2
[1. Shipwrecks—Fiction.   2. Babies—Fiction.   3. Sisters
4. Islands—Fiction.]   I. Sewell, Helen, date. ill.   II. Title.
PZ7.B78Bab   1993
[Fic]—dc20   92-45577
0614 OFF

Foreword

When I was a small girl, it was the fashion in our circle to borrow the neighbors' babies. I myself was never a very accomplished nursemaid, although I had many happy hours pushing the perambulator of a young cousin; but some of my friends had a positive genius for taking care of and amusing babies. They never thought of receiving pay for this delightful pastime. Minding a baby was its own reward.

It is more difficult to borrow babies now, I understand. Whether this is due to a scarcity of babies or to more particular mothers, I am unable to say. But I am quite sure of this: there are just as many little girls who love babies as there ever were, and it is especially for them that I have written the story of BABY ISLAND.

CAROL RYRIE BRINK

Contents

Contents

BABY ISLAND

CHAPTER ONE

The Wreck

ON THE night of September twentieth the *S.S. Orminta*, two weeks outward bound from San Francisco to Australia, was struck by a tropical storm and badly disabled. In the general panic which followed, nobody thought of the two little girls who were traveling alone to meet their father in Australia. But, although nobody remembered *her*, twelve-year-old Mary Wallace immediately thought of the babies. She was a motherly girl who was never so happy as when she had borrowed a baby to cuddle or care for.

So, when she woke up and found that the boat was sinking, she thought at once of the three Snodgrass babies. She dressed herself, shook her sister Jean and made her dress, and ran to help Mrs. Snodgrass rescue them. Jean, who was ten and a sound sleeper, followed her sister down the corridor with just one eye open and that open only part way. She had been dreaming that she had already reached Australia and was riding beside her father in a big red wagon. When Mary made her get up and dress and follow her through the corridor, she really didn't wake up at all, but

11

kept on dreaming that the wagon had broken down and that she was obliged to walk.

Mary, however, was as wide awake as a girl can be. She saw at once that she must be very quick if she were to help the Snodgrasses save their babies, for the big ocean liner was already tipping far over toward one side, and people were frantically rushing hither and thither in the darkness. Somewhere a woman was screaming, and the great engines deep inside the boat were pounding and throbbing terribly. Most girls of twelve would have been frightened, but Mary Wallace was not an ordinary girl. She made her way very coolly and deliberately to the far end of the boat, where Mr. Snodgrass, the Methodist field missionary, shared a large cabin with his wife and three babies. When she reached the cabin, she found the door open and the room apparently deserted.

"They are gone!" cried Mary, and she couldn't help feeling a little disappointed that they had not needed her help. "The babies are saved!"

But she had spoken too soon, for just then a feeble wail arose from one of the berths. Mary plunged into the dark cabin, calling: "Mrs. Snodgrass! Mr. Snodgrass! The boat is sinking!"

There was no response. Whether the missionary and his wife had gone for help or merely to ascertain the gravity

12

of the wreck, Mary did not know. But it became plain to her at once that, if the babies were to be saved, she must save them herself. She took Jonah, the very young Snodgrass baby up quickly, and wrapped him as warmly as possible in his blankets. Finding his half-emptied bottle of milk beside him, she wrapped it in the blanket with him, and thrust the whole bundle into the arms of sleepy Jean.

"Don't you dare to drop him, Jean," she cautioned.

"Do, I wod't," said Jean with a long sigh.

Then, wrapping the twins with the same hurried care, Mary took one under each arm, and, staggering under their

13

combined weight, made her way up on deck. There the first thing she saw was a group of frightened sailors who were hurriedly preparing a lifeboat. Without a moment's delay Mary presented herself before them and said, "Will you please save us?" The sailors readily did what they could for her, and Mary and the twins, the still-drowsy Jean and Jonah were securely installed in the small open boat.

"Oh," murmured Mary to herself, "if I only could have saved Ann Elizabeth, too! But, of course, she has two parents with only Ann Elizabeth and the white poodle to save, so she will probably be taken care of."

A great creaking windlass suddenly swung the lifeboat out over the side of the sinking vessel. They hung suspended in midair.

"Hey!" called a hoarse voice on the deck above, "don't let that boat down yet. She's not half full."

Mary's boat was drawn back toward the side of the vessel.

"Don't go without Mr. and Mrs. Snodgrass," called Mary, but her voice was entirely drowned by the noise of wind and wave and the shouting of the people on the steamer. The lifeboat swung back and forth in the wind like a hammockful of dolls. Jean had sunk down in the bottom of the boat in deep slumber, with the Snodgrass baby's head pillowed on her shoulder. Now she dreamed that they had reached the end of the journey and that she had at last been allowed to go to bed. Mary made the twins as comfortable as she could in the bottom of the boat, arranging a sort of bed and cover for them out of a large tarpaulin which she had found in the boat. Fortunately they were good sleepers and very calm. Then she kept her small, scared face turned toward the ship's railing looking for Mr. and Mrs. Snodgrass.

Presently someone whom she knew looked over the rail. It was neither the missionary nor his wife, but it was the father of Ann Elizabeth Arlington, the cutest baby on the steamship. Mr. Arlington's face looked very much frightened, but the sight of the half-empty boat seemed to give him courage. Then, seeing Mary, his face lost its anxious look entirely, and he cried: "Why, it's Mary Wallace! Here, will you just take Ann Elizabeth for a moment while I go back for Mrs. Arlington and the poodle? I am very much afraid that Mrs. Arlington has fainted. We'll be with you in just a moment."

Mary stretched out eager arms for Ann Elizabeth. Even if she was a teenty-weenty bit spoiled, she was the darlingest baby on the boat. The baby came smiling and cooing into Mary's arms, for Mary had often borrowed her in the happy days before the wreck; and with a sigh of relief Mr. Arlington disappeared on the deck of the great steamer. The wind howled; the waves crashed. Mary drew her last-winter's coat, which was a little too small this year, closer about her and Ann Elizabeth. She was growing more and more anxious for the Arlington and Snodgrass parents to come.

Suddenly there was a terrific crashing and creaking noise. Then in the stillness which followed, Mary heard a voice above her cry: "She's going to sink! Cast off the lifeboats!"

An instant later someone began lowering Mary's lifeboat. It struck the water with a splash, and bobbed there like a cork. For an instant it spun around and around, and Mary thought that it was going to be dashed against the side of the huge sinking steamer. But just then the wind and waves caught it and bore it safely away.

The great ship did not sink at once as the voice on deck had said that it would. For a long time Mary could see it with its lighted portholes tilted up at an odd angle. Then, as her little boat drifted swiftly away, fog and darkness closed in and the sinking ship was lost to view. At last Mary realized with a strange thrill that she and Jean were adrift on an unknown sea with a boatful of parentless babies. Seeing that there was nothing she could do about it, she settled down with her usual patience and good sense to get what pleasure she could out of the voyage, and to wait for whatever events the morrow would bring.

When the first flush of dawn broke over the troubled sea, Jean began to stir and waken. Her right arm and

16

shoulder were terribly lame from the weight of the youngest Snodgrass baby, and she had just been dreaming that she had been hunting and an Australian kangaroo had kicked her in the shoulder.

"Kesh kang-roo, Mary," she mumbled sleepily. "He's a'most killed me."

"There, there, Jeannie, you're only dreaming," said Mary kindly, reaching over the sleeping twins to pat Jean's shoulder.

Jean sat up and rubbed her eyes. She was tremendously surprised to find herself holding the Snodgrass baby. "Where am I?" she asked in a startled voice. For the first time since she had crawled into her berth on the big ocean liner the night before, she was wide awake.

"Well," said Mary, wishing to break it to her gently, "we're at sea, dear."

"Great fishes! I should think so!" said Jean, gazing about her at the miles and miles of water spread out on every side. "But how did we get here? I thought—"

"You see, Jean, there was a sort of a wreck," admitted Mary.

"A sort of a wreck?" repeated Jean with round eyes. "But how in the world—"

"We're in a lifeboat," said Mary. "Can't you remember how we rescued the babies and got in here and were lowered into the sea?"

17

Jean thought hard, but finally Mary had to tell her the whole story.

"But it's terrible, Mary," she said, when Mary had finished. "Why, what will the Snodgrasses and the Arlingtons do without their babies? And there is poor Father waiting for us in Australia and knowing very well that Aunt Emma put us on a boat. And most likely we'll perish at sea and never see any of them again." Jeannie began to fumble in her pockets for her handkerchief. Finally in desperation she took the blue one that always stuck out of the upper left-hand pocket of her coat. Mary was horrified.

"Oh, Jeannie!" she cried. "Don't cry on that! It's your best one that Aunt Emma gave you two years ago Christmas! Besides you mustn't cry at all. Do you suppose that Robinson Crusoe cried?"

"N-n-no," said Jean, "bu-bu-but I can't help it."

"Remember who you are," said Mary firmly. "Remember you're a Wallace. Sing 'Scots, Wha Hae wi' Wallace Bled' and you'll be all right."

"'*Scots, wha hae wi' Wallace bled!*'" sang Jean in a quavering voice.

"*Scots, wham Bruce has aften led,*
Welcome to your gory bed,
Or to victorie!
Now's the day an' now's the hour.

> *See the front of battle lour;*
> *See approach proud Edward's pow'r,*
> *Chains and slaverie!"*

"Well, go on," prompted Mary. "You don't look very cheerful yet."

Jeannie swung mournfully into the second verse:

> *"Wha would be a traitor knave?*
> *Wha would fill a coward's grave?*
> *Wha sae base as be a slave?*
> *Let him turn an' flee!*
> *Wha, for Scotland's king an' law,*
> *Freedom's sword would strongly draw,*
> *Freeman stand, and freeman fa',*
> *Let him on wi' me!"*

But Jeannie never reached the third stanza, for just then the tiny Snodgrass baby woke up and began to cry.

"I guess he doesn't like my singing," said Jean dolefully.

"Rock him," said Mary, "and let him have his thumb to suck. We'll have to spoil them a little in order to keep them quiet for a few days."

Jean obeyed, and the Snodgrass baby unwrinkled his little red face and went back to sleep with his thumb in his mouth. Jean began to cry softly again. "It's this terrible water," she said; "there's so much more of it than I ever thought there would be. Won't we ever see land again?"

"Now, Jean," said Mary firmly, "we've just got to be brave. I planned everything out last night while you were asleep and the boat was drifting along. Mr. Snodgrass was telling me only the other day that there are hundreds of little islands in this part of the sea, and I'm hoping to reach one before night."

"What makes you think so?"

"Because shipwrecked people always do," said Mary decidedly. "Why, the public library at home is just full of books about shipwrecked people who landed on tropical islands. And did you ever see a book written by a person who was drowned at sea? I never did."

Jean thought hard. "No," she said doubtfully, "but all I can say is, I wish we'd hurry up and get there."

"Goodness!" said Mary. "You can't expect everything to happen at once. Why, we just got wrecked last night. If Mr. Snodgrass said there were lots of little islands around here, there must be. You wouldn't catch a missionary making up a fib, Jeannie. I'm sure we're due at one of those islands right now. Of course, we *might* be a little late, like the Interurban cars used to be at home."

Jean gulped three times at all this sisterly good sense, and then she managed a bleak and watery smile.

The Lifeboat

THE sea grew more and more calm as the round southern sun came higher and higher above the horizon. A stiff breeze still carried the lifeboat forward; but the waves no longer crashed about it, hurling it hither and thither as they had in the night.

"The thing I'm most worried about is milk," said Mary, with a little pucker between her eyes. "When these babies wake up, they will want milk, and all I have is what's left in Jonah's bottle."

"In my pocket," said Jean, "I have the cake of milk cho'late that cousin Alex gave me before I left. I've been saving it for some special occasion. This *is* a special occasion, isn't it, Mary? Don't you wish you'd saved yours?"

"Yes," said Mary, "I do. But milk chocolate won't help the babies any. Do you s'pose they could live on cocoanut milk, Jean?"

"Wherever would you get the cocoanuts?"

"Why on the desert island, silly!"

Just then one of the Snodgrass twins sat up. Mary couldn't

21

tell whether he was Elijah or Elisha, because they were exactly alike. But this one had on a pink outing-flannel jacket, so Mary judged it to be Elisha or Pink as he was familiarly called. He was a fat baby nearly two years old. He wrinkled up his nose in a funny way and said, "Moo!"

"Oh, the funny rascal!" said Jean. "He thinks he's a cow."

The baby looked imploringly at Mary and stretched out his hands. "Me-me, moo," he entreated.

"The time has come," said Mary tragically.

He staggered to his feet and began to toddle unsteadily toward her. "Me-me, ba-ba moo," he said.

Mary knelt in the bottom of the boat and gathered him into her arms.

"What does he say?" asked Jean, who never understood babies quite so well as Mary did.

"He says, 'Mary, give baby some milk,'" translated Mary.

"What shall we do?" sighed Jean.

"Me-me no have moo," said Mary sadly, shaking her head at the baby.

"Mary Wallace, I'm ashamed of you," said Jean severely. "How many times have you heard Mr. Snodgrass say that the only way to help babies learn to talk is to speak to them sensibly as if they were grown-ups?"

"Well, what should I say?" asked Mary, on the verge of tears.

22

"Say: 'Elisha, we have no food at the present time, but with good luck and a fair wind we hope to land on a cocoanut island where you shall be fed.' "

At this speech Pink raised a terrible wail of protest.

"Now see what you've gone and done," said Mary.

Without a moment's delay the three other babies awoke and began to cry.

"Moo! Moo!" yelled the twins in chorus. The tiny Snodgrass baby sent up a thin, shrill wail, and Ann Elizabeth Arlington kicked her fat legs up and down and roared. Poor distracted Mary bent over one after another, comforting and caressing, but it was of no use. They were all hungry, and the best way they knew of getting food was to cry for it.

"I'm hungry, too," said Jean, putting her hand to her empty stomach. "Do you mind if I cry, too?"

"You can just bet I do!" replied her sister. "You must look around and see if you can find anything to eat."

"Yes," said Jean sarcastically, "if there's a bowl of soup or a strawberry shortcake hidden anywhere about, I'll be sure to find it."

"This is no time to joke, Jeannie Wallace. If you can't hunt for food, you can just jounce a few of these babies."

"I don't know which job is worse," said Jean, gazing dismally at the four crying babies, "but I guess I'll look for

23

food." She began to peer under seats and life preservers. Stowed neatly under the seat in the bow, she found two hatchets, a lantern, a can of oil, some blankets, a coil of rope, some canvas which looked as if it might be intended for a sail, a tin bucket, a canvas bucket, a wrench, some bailing tins, and a tin box of matches.

"What a lot of truck!" she exclaimed. "I s'pose the blankets may come in handy, but I'm sure that none of us want to drink the oil. It isn't even cod liver, and, goodness knows, that's about the worst kind there is."

"That oil must be for the lantern," said Mary. "Are you sure there isn't any food there, Jean?"

"Not a crumb to be seen," remarked Jean gloomily.

"Well, it's mighty queer," said Mary, giving a detachable oarlock to each of the twins and so for a moment quieting them. "It's mighty queer that they wouldn't put *something* to eat on a lifesaving boat, isn't it? They can't expect to save lives without any food, even if we did leave sort of unexpectedly."

But Jean did not answer at once, for she had just made a discovery. She was at the stern of the boat now, and she went down on her knees and began to rap on a wooden panel with her knuckles.

"Mary, I b'lieve there's a hollow place here at this end of the boat. I b'lieve this wooden panel must come out, and

24

that there must be some sort of cupboard inside. Come and help me!"

"Oh, I can't, Jean. The Blue Twin almost jumped overboard just now."

Jean stuck her fingers in the crack of the paneling and struggled manfully. "I see I'll have to be the father of this family," she said. Suddenly the panel came loose, and she toppled backward with the piece of wood in her hands. Inside the small cupboard space, which was thus revealed, were several neatly arranged rows of tin boxes and cans.

"What is it?" called Mary over the terrific howling of the four babies, which was growing worse every minute. Jean regained her balance and began to investigate.

25

"Two jugs of water," she called. "That'll be something for them to drink."

"Water! Oh, dear! Are you sure it isn't milk?"

"Sure. And hardtack. Ugh! I hate hardtack."

"But, Jean," cried Mary delightedly, "hardtack will be the very thing for the babies to cut their teeth on!"

"Canned beans," continued Jean, "and canned beef."

"Not so good," said Mary, "the babies can't digest such heavy food."

"Believe me," said Jean, *"I can."* She was busy pulling out cans. Suddenly she gave a shout and waved a can in the air.

"Canned milk!" she screamed. "Canned milk!"

"What?" cried Mary, beaming with joy and almost unable to believe her ears. "Canned milk?"

"Moo! Moo!" shrieked the Snodgrass twins, tumbling over each other to try to reach Jean. Jean triumphantly produced a can opener and several tin cups, and began to prepare the babies' breakfast.

"Oh," said Mary, "it's too good to be true. I never was so pleased to find anything in my life." In a moment Mary knew exactly what to do. "Light the lantern, Jean, and mix some of the water and the milk together in a cup and warm it over the lantern."

26

This was a rather slow process, but while the milk was warming, Jean beguiled the time with an oration.

"The hen that laid this milk—" she began dramatically, flourishing a can.

"Be sensible, Jean," said Mary, laughing. "Hens don't lay milk."

"Well, what I mean to say is, the cow that gave this milk shall have my internal gratitude."

"You mean 'eternal gratitude,'" corrected Mary. "We mustn't forget our grammar just because we've become sailors, Jean."

The twins were able to feed themselves without spilling more than a fourth of each cup, and Jean held the cup for Ann Elizabeth, who began to smile and gurgle as soon as she tasted the milk. Mary reserved for herself the more difficult task of feeding the tiny Snodgrass baby. How glad she was now that she had thought to bring his bottle!

"We should never have been able to teach him to drink out of a cup, Jean!"

"I've seen Cousin Alex teach a young calf to drink by putting his finger down in the milk pail and letting the calf suck his finger," remarked Jean.

"But Mrs. Snodgrass was always so particular about having everything boiled and sanitary and not touching any-

27

thing with her fingers. It would have been awful to do it that way."

"Well, it never killed the calf," observed Jean, as she wiped Ann Elizabeth's mouth and nose on a corner of the tarpaulin.

Finally all the hungry babies were fed, and Mary laid Jonah in the bottom of the boat on her folded coat. The sun had become delightfully warm, and he soon went to sleep again. Ann Elizabeth, her head wreathed in shiny curls, sat up sedately and played with her fingers. The twins were more trouble, for everything small which they could lay hands on must be put in their mouths, and everything too large to go in their mouths must be thrown overboard. Jean just caught the Blue Twin in time as he was about to hurl one of the precious cans of milk into the sea. They had already thrown over all the detachable oarlocks, and Mary remarked with a sigh that the mermaids down below would certainly know that the Snodgrass twins were going by, by the number of loose objects which were thrown down.

"Well, it's *something* not to be *able* to pick the things up again," said Jean. "Do you remember how the twins used to fling the knives and forks and spoons off the table fifty times during a meal on the steamship? I used to get a cramp in my back helping poor Mrs. Snodgrass pick them up."

"This *will* be something of a vacation for poor Mrs.

28

Snodgrass," said Mary thoughtfully. "I hope she's where she can enjoy it."

Finally Jean thought of providing the twins with pieces of hardtack, which kept them happy for some time. The girls opened a can of beef.

"I like milk, too," hinted Jeannie in a gentle voice.

"Jean," said Mary severely, "we are parents now, and parents must always think first of their children. These babies will need every speck of that milk."

"Yes'm," said Jean humbly, reaching for the canned beef.

In this moment of comparative quiet the two girls from the United States began to take stock of their belongings and plan for the future. They were very independent and self-reliant little girls, for, ever since they could remember, they had had to do almost everything for themselves. Their mother had died when they were quite small, and their father, although a very kind man, had been too busy making a living for them to lavish much attention upon them. There had been housekeepers, of course, but it was always wise little Mary who took the responsibility of the household. When Mary was ten, their father had been offered the management of a big ranch in Australia. He did not wish to take his children to such a faraway country until he was sure that he liked it and wished to settle there. So for two years Mary and Jean had lived with Aunt Emma,

29

Uncle Angus, and grown-up Cousin Alex in Scotsville, Iowa.

In Scotsville they had never had time to be lonely. They went to school, of course, and there was a great deal to do to help Aunt Emma, and, after school and chores were done, they went out and borrowed the neighbors' babies. They played with them, and wheeled them and jounced them and put them to sleep. The tired and work-worn mothers of Scotsville considered Mary and Jean nature's greatest blessings, the babies loved them, and Mary and Jean themselves were perfectly happy.

At the end of the two years, their father had sent for them, and with many tears at parting, Aunt Emma had put them on the train that would take them to San Francisco. There they had been met by another relative who had put them on the steamship *Orminta.* For nearly two weeks they had had a most delightful time, wandering about her decks, making friends with the captain, and most of all helping Mrs. Snodgrass and Mrs. Arlington with their babies. Then came the wreck, and now, of course, they were obliged to change all their plans for the future. For here they were with four babies to care for in an open boat, and the prospect of reaching their father in Australia seemed now very dim.

"It's too bad you didn't bring along some of our baggage, Mary," said Jean regretfully.

"Good gracious! I had all I could do to rescue the twins and you and Jonah. I didn't have time to think of toothbrushes and nightgowns."

"Well, I don't feel so bad about toothbrushes," said Jean. "But what I do feel bad about is my pink taffeta—the only silk dress I ever had, and now it's gone to the bottom of the sea! I'm afraid the fish won't 'preciate it."

"Never mind," consoled Mary. "Just think how sweet a baby whale would look in it, Jeannie."

"And there's Miranda," continued Jean plaintively. "She's the best doll I ever had, even if her skull is cracked and her front teeth knocked out."

"Goodness," said Mary. "I shouldn't feel sorry about that dreadful old doll, if I were you. Here we have four live ones. As long as I can remember we've had to borrow other people's babies. It's a perfect shame the way we've had to go around and beg and borrow, and say, 'Please, ma'am, may we take your baby out?' And then we could only keep 'em a half an hour or so. Now we have four, and they're *ours!* We ought to be the happiest girls in the world!"

Jean nodded vigorously. Her mouth was too full of canned beef to reply.

THE LIFEBOAT

CHAPTER THREE

A Wild Night

WHILE the babies napped and the lifeboat bobbed over the waters, Mary and Jean turned out their pockets to see what useful things chance might have sent along with them. Out of Jean's came a ball of string, a piece of tinfoil, a chain of safety pins, a stubby pencil, and a half-written postal card for Aunt Emma.

"There's no use in *that* anyway," said Mary, looking at the card.

It was a picture of the *Orminta*, floating upon a calm blue sea. On the other side, Jean had written:

Dear Aunt: The wether is fine. We are all fine. This is a fine boat.

"Oh, what fibs!" exclaimed Jean.

"They're not fibs at all," said Mary, smiling, "only the picture on the other side ought to show our lifeboat instead of the steamer. For the weather really is fine today, we are all well, and this is a fine boat even if it is a very little one."

Jean was already busy filling up the rest of the space on the card. She wrote:

A WILD NIGHT

We are on our way to a dessert iland with the Snodgrass babies and Ann Elizabeth Arlington. We are all well and happy, hoping you are the same.

Your luving neece,

Jean.

P.S. The boat in the picture was recked. We are in a fine little lifeboat.

"I promised Aunt Emma I'd write her every week," said Jean solemnly, "so here goes number one by deep-water express." She wrote her aunt's name and address on the card, folded it several times, wrapped it in the piece of tinfoil, put it in the empty beef can, bent down the cover, and set the can floating across the water.

"Well, of all things!" said Mary. "I suppose you expect the postman to come by and collect it."

"No," admitted Jean, "but Aunt Emma can't say I didn't try, can she?"

The two girls laughed, but somehow their laughter wasn't very mirthful, for they kept thinking of Aunt Emma's sorrowful face when she would hear of the wreck and receive no news of them.

Mary's pockets were always more orderly than Jean's. She had a small purse with a few coins in it, a very neat notebook with a calendar in the back, and a "housewife." The housewife was a small leather case containing a pair of scissors, a thimble, thread, and needles, which Mary

33

declared would be very useful in keeping the babies' clothes tidy.

"And it's lucky I have this notebook, too," she said, "for the calendar will help us keep track of time, and that's important. If we didn't have a calendar, we might forget when Sunday comes, and the babies must be brought up to respect the Sabbath day and keep it holy, just as they would if they were at home."

"But we can't go to Sunday school on a desert island," objected Jean.

"No," replied Mary, "but we can lay aside our labors and sing a hymn, and you can repeat the twenty-third Psalm to the children so's you won't forget it."

Jean heaved a heavy sigh. The twenty-third Psalm had always been a great trial to her.

"And in the rest of the notebook," Mary continued, "we'll make a record, like a family Bible." Taking the pencil, Mary sat with it poised for a moment, lost in thought. Then on the first page of the notebook, she wrote in a clear round hand the following record:

Elisha (Pink) Elijah (Blue)	aged 20 months	sons of Rev. Jonah E. Snodgrass, missionary, and his wife, Edith
Jonah	aged 4 months	
Ann Elizabeth	aged 1 year	daughter of Mr. Christopher Arlington, lawyer, and his wife, Rebecca

A WILD NIGHT

Rescued from the sinking ship *Orminta* by

Mary	aged 12	⎫ daughters of Sandy Wallace, manager
and		⎬ of the Prince Charley Ranch, Aus-
Jean	aged 10	⎭ tralia

SHIP'S LOG

Sept. 21—At sea—expect to reach a desert island soon.

But in spite of their hopes of reaching a desert island, the day wore slowly on with not a glimpse of land. During the hottest hours, they stretched the tarpaulin over one end of the boat as a shelter for the babies, who really seemed to be enjoying the adventure. They had become so attached to Mary and Jean on board ship that now they scarcely missed their mothers at all. So much sun and fresh air made them sleepy, and, while they dozed, Mary and Jean washed out such of their garments as needed attention and dried them on oars stretched across the boat. As she worked, Jean made up a song, and this is what she sang:

> "Oh, there wasn't enough water in all the land
> To wash out the clothes of Elizabeth Ann;
> And Mary and Jean, they couldn't get
> Water enough to make them wet;
> And the Snodgrass twins had got so black
> We had to feed 'em on old hardtack.
> But Mary and Jean they thought of a plan
> (They always do as fast as they can);

35

They took the babies out on the sea
And everything there was as wet as could be;
So the babies got clean as a new penn-y.
Oh, Mary and Jean are very smart girls
(Although they have never had hair that curls).
Oh, Jean is espeshully very smart,
She learned the twenty-third Psalm by heart.
And now they are traveling many a mile
To get to a beautiful desert isle!"

Toward evening the waves began to grow rough again, and the girls looked anxiously up at the sky, wondering what the night had in store for them.

"The Interurban car at home was never this late, Mary," Jean declared.

"Never mind," said Mary, trying to look cheerful. "We'll get to land soon—I'm sure we will. Don't you remember I told you it was only the other day (though it seems a year ago) that Mr. Snodgrass told me this part of the ocean is full of little nameless islands? Why, he said there were so many tiny ones they couldn't even make a map of them."

"Just the same, I wish somebody *had* made a map of them," Jean said, "and then we'd find out where we are and steer for the nearest land. Ooh! but my legs need stretching!"

"So do mine," admitted Mary. "But without a map, there's no use trying to steer. Because for all we know we might be steering ourselves just the very wrongest way. I'm going to sit right here a while longer and keep hoping the wind knows where it's taking us."

The sun went down with flaming colors, and a strange, clear twilight hung over the sea for a long time. It made the sky and sea look much vaster, and the girls felt small and alone as they bobbed up and down on the waves. When the sun was gone it began to grow cold, and they were glad for the blankets which they had found in the boat.

Ann Elizabeth cried a little, because her mother, having only her and the poodle to look after, had always rocked her to sleep at night. But the Snodgrass babies were used to going to bed under all sorts of strange conditions, and they went to sleep at once. Mary and Jean curled themselves together in the middle of the boat to snatch some rest. They were tired after the adventures of the previous night and the long day in the open boat. Jean fell asleep at once, and tired Mary was just beginning to doze when a long, mournful wail from Jonah brought her up with a jump. The youngest Snodgrass baby's face was screwed into a knot of misery. He drew up his knees against his stomach and clutched and clawed with his tiny pink hands. Mary took him up with little cries of pity. But no gentle words could persuade him, and neither rocking nor jouncing did any good. Mary began to be frightened. He was evidently in

37

great misery, and it wrung Mary's heart to see him suffer and not be able to help him.

"Wake up, Jean," she cried. "You've got to help me. Oh, I do wish I knew what is the matter with him!"

Jean sat up and rubbed her eyes. "Sheashick," she muttered.

"Oh, no, surely not seasick," worried Mary. "Babies don't know whether they're upside down or right side up. So how could he be seasick!"

"Colic!" Jean said next.

Mary was struck by this remark, even though she knew that Jean was half asleep when she made it.

"What makes you think it's colic?"

"Mishush Schnodgrash," mumbled Jean.

"That's right!" said Mary, thinking rapidly. "I've heard Mrs. Snodgrass say it myself. 'Jonah is subject to the colic,' she said, 'if his milk doesn't agree with his stomach or if a cold draught blows on his head.' Goodness knows, the poor lamb has had enough cold draughts on his head today, and there's no telling how this canned milk agrees with his stomach. It must be the colic!"

"Whatsh colic?" asked Jean, beginning to take a sleepy interest in things.

"It's a terrible stomachache, that's what it is!" said Mary, cuddling the screaming baby.

38

"Too bad you couldn't have let me sleep, Mary," grumbled Jean. "Listening to him howl isn't going to help *him* any, and it certainly hurts *me* a lot."

"Oh, Jean! Aren't you ashamed? Think now! See if you can remember what Mrs. Snodgrass does for the colic."

Jean tried hard, but every time she began to remember she dozed off to sleep.

"It's no good," she said at last, "my thinker's gone to bed."

"Oh, dear!" sighed Mary. "I don't know if colic is ever fatal, but he's certainly got an awful case. Oh, I wish Mrs. Snodgrass were here!" For some time poor Mary rocked and struggled with the unhappy baby. Then she decided to heat some water over the lantern. She handed the squalling baby to Jean, who took him in a daze, holding him gingerly at arm's length.

"Of coursh you know what they did to Jonah in the Bible, Mary," she remarked.

Mary was too busy trying to warm her water to pay much attention to Jean's remark. "What did they do?" she asked. "I hope it was a good cure for colic."

"I guess it was," said Jean. "You know there was an awful storm, and the ship was about to be wrecked, and the sailors prayed to the Lord to save them, and He said, 'I will save you, if you'll throw Jonah overboard.' And they did, and He did, and the storm ceased."

39

"I don't see what that has to do with colic."

"Yes, but it had a lot to do with Jonah. Maybe if the captain of the *Orminta* had thrown Jonah Snodgrass overboard in time, we wouldn't be out here now floating around in a lifeboat."

"Jean!" shouted Mary. "You aren't thinking of throwing Jonah overboard?"

"Well, it's an idea," said Jean.

Mary gave a little scream and caught the baby out of Jean's arms. In her excitement she flung him sharply against her shoulder.

40

"Glub! glub!" said Jonah, with a gasp and gurgle like air escaping from a toy balloon. Immediately he stopped howling. Mary was so alarmed at this sudden silence that she felt sure she must have killed him. But, when the moon came struggling out of the clouds, she discovered that he was looking at her with calm round eyes and peacefully sucking his thumb.

"Oh, Jean!" she cried, "he's coughed up his misery!"

Just then the cup of water, which she had set on top of the lantern, began to bubble, and in a moment she had succeeded in giving him a little warm water. He cried fitfully for half an hour after that, but now Mary was no longer worried. She knew how to put him against her shoulder and pat his back until he gulped up the troublesome gas. Presently he fell asleep, and it seemed as if the waves of the sea and all the stars in the firmament had suddenly grown calm now that Jonah had ceased to howl. Much relieved, Mary put him snugly to bed and looked around to see what had become of Jean. All she could see was a dark bunch in the bottom of the boat. Jean had melted into a heap of slumber just where she sat.

Several days later Mary asked Jean if she remembered wanting to throw Jonah into the sea. Jean looked at her in indignant surprise.

"Why, Mary," she said, "you must have been dreaming!"

41

CHAPTER FOUR

Bananas!

AFTER her troubled night, Mary slept late next morning. When she woke at last, the sun was shining brightly. It dazzled her for a moment and she couldn't think where she was. Something strange had been happening to her for the last few days, but she couldn't quite remember. Then somewhere in the distance she heard Jean singing one of her made-up songs, and somebody was tugging at her sleeve. She opened her eyes wider and found herself gazing into the earnest round face of the Pink Twin. Then Mary remembered that she was at sea in a lifeboat with Mrs. Snodgrass' twins. When the Pink Twin saw her awake, he began to bounce himself up and down with excitement.

"Bye-bye, Me-me, bye-bye!" he exclaimed.

"Darling thing," said Mary, trying to kiss him, "we can't go bye-bye."

But he wriggled from her embrace, and pointed a dramatic finger, crying: "Bye-bye! Me-me, ba-ba bye-bye!"

Suddenly a tremendous idea flashed into Mary's mind. The boat was no longer moving! She could hear the waves lapping against it, but the boat itself was quite still. With a little cry, she sprang up and gazed about her. To her astonishment she saw that they were safely lodged on a sandy shore, just at the edge of the dancing, sparkling waves. She could see a long stretch of shining sand, and then a fringe of graceful palm trees and vegetation. Running in and out among the first of these trees, she could see Jean, gleefully capering, shouting, and singing.

Mary sat down again, perfectly flabbergasted.

"Well," she gasped, "we got here!" Then she added fervently, "Oh, thank you, Lord!"

Ann Elizabeth and Jonah were still asleep. The Blue Twin had clambered over the side of the boat and was toddling after Jean. The Pink Twin still pulled at Mary's skirt and cried, "Bye-bye! bye-bye! bye-bye!"

"All right, Pink," cried Mary happily. "I don't know how we got here, but we aren't going to let Jean and Elijah beat us. No siree!" Casting a glance at the sleeping babies, she caught Pink up under her arm and ran after the other twin, who had fallen on his nose in the soft sand.

"Oh, twinsies!" she said, setting them both right side up again. "What a wonderful sandpile! Aren't you the lucky babies!" The twins may not have understood her words, but they understood her happy tone of voice, for they clapped their fat hands and squealed with delight. "Just see," she went on, catching up handfuls of the sand, "what castles we can make. I guess not even the richest millionaire in America has such a sandpile as this in *his* backyard for *his* babies!"

Pink began digging like a little dog, throwing the sand out behind, between his fat legs, and Blue amused himself by pouring sand in his hair and chuckling with delight when it ran tickling down the back of his neck.

Just then Jean came running from the group of trees, shouting at the top of her voice and waving something yellow which she held in her hands.

"What is it, Jean?" called Mary, preparing to pick up the babies and run if any danger threatened.

"Bananas!" cried Jean, waving her arms as she ran.

> *Bananas! bananas! bananas!*
> *I'm singing hosannas*
> *'Cause I've found bananas!*
> *Bananas! bananas! bananas!"*

"Really?" asked Mary, incredulously.

"Really!" said Jean, all out of breath, dropping down on the sand beside them. She exhibited half a dozen large yellow bananas. "The trees are full of them. Oh, I never hoped to find such a heavenly place on earth! Think of having all the bananas you want to eat! That's almost like picking caramels off bushes."

"Oh, yum!" said Mary. "I like bananas, too."

"Nana! nana!" cried the twins, reaching sandy fingers.

Jean distributed the fruit. The twins instantly began to pull off the skins and stuff the ripe fruit into their mouths.

"Dear me!" said Mary weakly. "I don't know what Mrs. Snodgrass would say. Bananas before breakfast! Isn't that supposed to be terrible for the digestion?"

"Oh, let them, just this once," begged Jean. "Today we ought to celebrate because we've reached our island."

"However did we get here, Jean? Did you see us arrive?"

"No, I was asleep, too. But I felt a sort of gentle bump and a grating on sand, and then we stopped moving, and I woke up and here we were. I sat up and looked around. You and the babies kept right on sleeping as if nothing had happened, and at first I thought maybe I was having one of my nightmares, only it was really too pleasant to be a nightmare. I started to wake you up, and then I thought: 'Gracious! somebody's always yanking me out of a nice, cosy sleep, and that makes me cross. I'll let poor Mary sleep it out. We'll probably be here long enough, anyway!' "

"Well, I *was* surprised," declared Mary, "and I expect you're right about our being here a long time. It certainly does look like a desert island, if I ever saw one. We'll have to begin exploring right after breakfast, and then we'll have to set up housekeeping somewhere. We've got the babies to think of, you know."

"What shall we name our new country? Bananaland?" Jean was already beginning on her fifth banana.

"How about Babyland?" suggested Mary. "You and I will be king and queen, and all our subjects babies."

"We do seem to be terribly mixed up with babies," admitted Jean. "How about calling this place Baby Island? For, of course, it's an island or we wouldn't have come bumping into it the way we did right out in the middle of the ocean."

46

"All right," said Mary. "I like that name. Baby Island it shall be!"

Just then from the boat they heard Ann Elizabeth's voice, crying for breakfast. Her lusty cry was immediately joined by Jonah's shrill wail, making a sort of alto and soprano duet.

"Our subjects are calling us," said Mary, starting to run.

"You're all mixed up, Mary," laughed Jean, as she ran to help her sister. "We're not the king and queen of Baby Island—we're the slaves!"

The girls made a hasty breakfast in the boat, for they were both in a hurry to begin exploring. But first of all there was a certain amount of housework to be done. There was washing, and the babies all needed baths.

"First let's pull the boat as far up on shore as we can," said Mary, "so that a sudden wind won't carry it out to sea. We can let the babies roll around on the sand until we get that done."

So they left the babies rolling and tumbling in the clean sand, while they went at the task of pulling the boat ashore. This was hard to do, for the boat was heavy. Bobbing on the open sea, it had often seemed small, but now that they had it on the beach, it seemed as heavy and unwieldy as a dead elephant. But the two girls pulled and pushed with all their strength, working it inch by inch up onto the dry sand.

"Whew!" remarked Jean, wiping the perspiration from her forehead. "That was some job!"

"I know," said Mary, "and that's not the last hard thing we'll have to do before we leave this island. But we won't let anything beat us, Jean. A Wallace never gives up."

"No, sir!" said Jean. "Never!" And the two young Wallaces ground their teeth and gave the boat a last triumphant tug.

"Now we'll make a tent," announced Mary.

Searching among the piles of driftwood which lay here and there along the beach, the girls found two long sticks, and stuck them deep into the sand a short distance from the boat. To these two poles they fastened two corners of the tarpaulin which had already been so useful to them in the boat. The other two corners were fastened to the side of the boat, so that it formed a sort of tent with the side of the lifeboat as a sheltering wall at the back. At first they had some difficulty in fastening the tarpaulin securely, but by twisting the corners of it around the stakes and using Jean's safety pins to fasten it tightly in place, they managed to get a good, firm anchorage.

"Maybe that's not the way a seaman would do it," said Mary, sitting back on her heels to admire the result. "But I call that a pretty fine tent."

48

"Oh, Mary, I'm sorry to interrupt you," said Jean, "but Ann Elizabeth is eating sand. Do you suppose we gave her enough breakfast?"

"Oh, Ann Elizabeth, no! No!" cried Mary, running to the rescue. "It's nasty! 'Pit it out. 'Pit it out right away. Oh, Jean, get the water jug and we'll wash her mouth out."

"The dirty baby! And there you go talking baby talk to her!" exclaimed Jean disapprovingly. But she fetched the water jug just the same. Ann Elizabeth seemed to enjoy the sand very much, for she said, "Goo-goo," and reached for more.

"Poor darling! She doesn't know any better," apologized Mary tenderly, as she cleaned the squirming baby's mouth. After washing Ann Elizabeth's mouth, she picked up the water jug, weighing it carefully in her hands. She tried to peer inside it, but the earthenware neck was too small to allow her to see how much water was left.

"You know this water isn't going to last forever," she said dubiously. "The next thing we must do is to hunt for fresh water, and, when we find it, we must build our house near it. Folks can't get along without water."

"Isn't there any way of using sea water, Mary?"

"No. It is so salty, it would just make us thirstier and thirstier. If we can't get fresh water, we'll all die."

"Oh, dear," said Jean. "I'd hate to die now, Mary, just

when I've found all the bananas I want to eat! I always did like bananas better than water."

"Yes," continued Mary, "as soon as we can get the babies all asleep for their naps, we must go exploring for a stream of water. It's very important. But first we will give them their baths."

"Oh, Mary," cried Jean, laughing, "the Blue Twin has taken his already. Just look at him!"

During the excitement of washing out Ann Elizabeth's mouth, the Blue Twin had escaped the girls' watchful eyes, and gone down to the sea. There he was splashing and paddling to his heart's content. The beach sloped so gradually into the water that there was no danger, and he squealed with joy as the little frothy ripples splashed over him. The Pink Twin stood on the shore clapping his hands at his brother's antics, and ready at any moment to plunge in himself.

"Wa-wa!" he cried happily. "Ba-ba, wa-wa!"

Mary caught him just before he splashed in beside Elijah. "You hold Pink, while I dry Blue," said Mary. "We must never, never mix them!"

"They are so much alike that I don't see what difference it would make, if we did mix 'em up," objected Jean.

"Really," said Mary, "I think that's rather heartless, Jean. It wouldn't somehow be honest to Mrs. Snodgrass to put a pink shirt on Elijah and call him Elisha, nor to put the blue shirt on Elisha and call him Elijah, because she intended it the other way around."

"Oh, pouf!" said Jean. But just the same she knew that Mary was right.

Mary stripped Elijah and hung his blue-edged shirt and nightie to dry on the boat. Then she proceeded to give him a bath as well as she could without soap, sponge, or towel. The towel was really not greatly needed, because the warm sun so readily dried him.

"But I do wish I had a good cake of castile soap," said Mary, "and a can of talcum powder. I suppose that babies *can* be raised without the use of talcum powder, but I've never heard of its being done."

"This sand is nice and fine—" suggested Jean.

"Oh, Jean," said Mary in despair, "you can't compare sand with a nice baby talcum—*ever!*"

"I s'pose not," said Jean sadly.

When Elijah's blue clothes were well dried, he was dressed again, and then Jean undressed the Pink Twin and let him splash, while she and Mary bathed Ann Elizabeth and Jonah. The three older babies felt so lively after their baths that Jean asked Mary if she might have a circus with them in the new tarpaulin tent. Mary, busy preparing Jonah's milk and getting him ready for his long

51

nap, readily consented. So Jean spread a blanket on the sand under the shelter, and crawled in with the three babies. At first she played that she was a lion and crept around, growling and snarling, to the great delight of the twins who pulled her hair and squealed with happiness. Then they wanted to be lions themselves and growl and tumble about, so Jean turned herself into an elephant and took Ann Elizabeth riding on her back. It was a very gay and successful circus, and gave the babies such an appetite for dinner that Mary began to wonder how much longer the milk supply was going to hold out. After they had eaten, the fat little things simply toppled over asleep in a state of happy exhaustion.

"Aren't they darling?" cried Jean. "Let's leave them just where they are."

"No, I think that we'd better put them in the boat," said Mary. "If anything should happen, they would be better off there."

So the girls tucked them in as carefully as they could, and, with a last anxious look at them, they hurried away on their tour of exploration.

CHAPTER FIVE

Time and Tide

THE girls went along the beach, because, as Mary said, if there was a stream anywhere on the island it would be sure to run down to the sea. Besides, they could go more quickly and safely on the beach than in the tangled undergrowth of the inner island.

"I hate awfully to go and leave the babies alone like this," said Mary, as they hastened along, "but it seems the only way."

"Yes," said Jean, "we shouldn't get along very fast carrying four fat babies. It's too bad we didn't get shipwrecked with a nice automobile or at least a pony and cart. But shipwrecks are so unexpected, you never know what you're going to need until it's too late."

They soon forgot everything else in wonder and admiration, as new stretches of beach opened out before them. A short distance from the spot where their boat had landed, a ridge of rocks broke through the sand and straggled down into the sea. When they had clambered on top of this, they could see more beach and rocks ahead, and here and there clumps of palm trees leaning out toward the sea.

"There ought to be cocoanuts in those palm trees, if I remember my geography," said Mary, "but dear, oh, dear! the trunks are so tall and slippery-looking, I don't know how we'll ever get them."

About their feet in the crevices of the rocks were little pools of sea water, and Jean often exclaimed over some funny crab or sea creature.

"Oh, Mary," she cried, "do you suppose that we could find clams for a clambake? Or lobsters Newburg, or finnan haddie, or something like that?"

"I expect so," said Mary. "Nothing would surprise me now that we are on a desert island."

The sun grew hotter as they went along, and it seemed as if they had walked miles before they saw anything but sand and rocks and sea. At last, however, they saw yellow cliffs rising at the edge of the beach.

"Well, they look *different* anyway! Let's run for them and see what we can find."

They raced along the beach until they reached the cliffs and dropped down, panting, in the welcome shade of over-hanging rocks.

"I have an idea," said Mary. "Do you see that turn in the cliffs right ahead? We can't see what's around that corner, so let's make a game of it. Let's shut our eyes when we get to the turn, and walk ten steps without looking. Then we'll open our eyes and see what we find. We have been lucky so far—perhaps we'll be lucky again."

So, forgetting their weariness, the two girls got up again and went to the turn in the cliffs. Just before they got to the place where they would be able to look around the bend and see what was ahead of them, they closed their eyes, took hold of hands, and started forward across the smooth sand. One—two—three—four—five (ouch! Jean stubbed her toe, but she didn't open her eyes)—six—seven —eight—nine—ten—open! They both looked about them. There was no sound or sight of babbling brook, but in the side of the cliff was something which made them forget their need of water in the excitement of discovery.

"It's a cave, Mary!"

"Jean, it's a cave!"

They caught each other about the waist and executed a couple of dizzy whirls.

When they had sobered down a little, Jean asked, "Do we dare go in?"

"Of course, we do."

"It looks pretty dark and scary."

"I guess William Wallace wouldn't have been scared."

The two girls went softly over to the mouth of the cave,

tiptoeing as if they expected to find something lurking within. But, when their eyes grew accustomed to the shadows, it seemed to be quite empty. It had a smooth sand floor that looked as if it had just been scrubbed. They stepped across the threshold, and suddenly the noise of the sea on the beach seemed much farther away. It gave them a cosy feeling of security.

"Jean," said Mary, "maybe we could live here."

The clean sand floor stretched back some distance to a rough, irregular wall. They had to stoop a little to enter, but once inside they could easily stand erect.

"It's kind of clammy," said Jean.

"Yes, it is. It might give Jonah the colic."

"That would be awful!"

"But, at least," said Mary, "we'd have a roof over our heads, and a cool shelter from the sun in the hot part of the day."

"I wish it had a drinking fountain in it," said Jean.

"You're right, Jean—we haven't found our fresh water yet, have we? But I believe that we have gone as far as we ought to go today. We have enough water in the jug to last a few more days if we are careful. Let's go back to the babies now."

It seemed a longer way back than it had been to come, but there was so much to talk about that they chattered gayly as they went along. Mary was full of housewifely plans for the furnishing of their new home, and Jean began making up one of her nonsense songs.

> *"Oh, I'm going to rave*
> *About a cave*
> *We found on Baby Island!*
> *It's nice and warm*
> *In case of storm,*
> *And Jean and Mary found it!*
> *Oh, Jean and Mary live in caves*
> *Because they're Baby Island slaves,*
> *And they rode on the billowy, willowy waves*
> *To get to Baby Island."*

Suddenly Jean stopped singing and said: "Why, Mary, the beach isn't as wide as it was when we came by here before! I remember this place in partic'lar. Why, I believe the sea's getting higher."

"How could it?" said Mary.

"But, Mary, it has! Where are the little pools that we saw among the rocks? And where are the tracks we made in the sand when we came by here before?"

"You are right!" said Mary, with a sudden chill of fear. "We are walking just as near the sea as we did before, but we're walking higher up."

"Yes, sir," cried Jean emphatically, "the water has covered our tracks, Mary. Oh, what do you suppose makes it?"

Suddenly Mary began to run. "I know what it is! It's the tide! Oh, it's the tide coming in, and the babies are alone! Oh, my darling babies!"

"The tide?" gasped Jean.

Running behind Mary, she tried to remember what she had read about the tide in the big geography at school. The moon was like a big magnet, she remembered, drawing the water of the oceans toward itself and causing the ebb and flow of tides on beaches the world around. But she had never thought how terrible it would be to see it come, each wave rushing a little farther as if it meant to swallow the land altogether. There was something about it in her old grammar book, too. *Time and tide wait for no man,* that was what it said. And the babies! Four little babies alone in a boat that had been high and dry when they left it. Where would it be now?

The girls wasted no more breath on talking. They put all their strength into running as they had never run before. Panting and stumbling over rocks and sand, they somehow managed to keep going. Such a long way it seemed now. Why had they come so far and left the babies alone? Jean needed to sing "Scots, Wha' Hae wi' Wallace Bled" very much just now, but even more she needed her breath and strength for running. Mary's legs were a little longer than hers, and, like time and tide, Mary waited for no man. It was all that Jean could do to keep up with her.

At last they saw ahead of them the ridge of rock that jutted down into the sea. On the other side of that was the beach where they had left the babies. Mary gave a little groan of anguish and relief. It was a relief to see that they were almost there, and yet she was so frightened that she scarcely dared look to see if the babies were safe. She scrambled to the top of the ridge of rock and paused there an instant, crying hoarsely: "There! There they are, Jean."

Jean looked, too, for a fleeting instant before she began to rush down the other side. The boat, which they had struggled so valiantly to pull high and dry on the beach that morning, was floating far out in the water. It was bobbing gently with every wave that came in, but something seemed to keep it anchored in one spot.

"It's the tarp," gasped Mary. "The good old tarpaulin has anchored it!"

"And my safety pins!" croaked Jean.

Sure enough, the stakes which they had driven deep in the sand that morning still stood firm, and the tarpaulin tent held the boat safely moored to the stakes, so that it couldn't drift out to sea.

As they drew nearer they heard a chorus of shouts from the frightened babies. For a moment the two girls paused at the water's edge, wondering what to do. Then Mary Wallace stepped out into the frothy water and began splashing and floundering through the waves toward the boat.

"Mary, you know you can't swim!" warned Jean in a frightened voice. But nothing could stop Mary now until her babies were safe. The twins saw her coming, and began to bounce themselves about, shouting, "Me-me, me-me!"

"Me-me is coming, darlings!" she called.

Then the Blue Twin remembered how he had climbed over the side of the boat to follow Jean that morning, and, seeing his beloved "Me-me" coming, he decided to try it again. Jean saw him swinging his fat legs over the side of the boat, and screamed a warning to Mary. Then, *splash!* he had lost his balance and toppled over the side into the water. The water was up to Mary's armpits as she reached the boat, but she ducked down after Blue and finally brought him up to the surface. The anxious Jean saw them reappear, coughing and spluttering and dripping wet, Mary holding the twin aloft by a piece of his blue-trimmed jacket. As soon as Mary could get her breath and shake the water out of her eyes, she tumbled him back into the boat, and, wrenching the tarpaulin from the stakes which had held it, she began to tow the boat back to shore.

60

Jean splashed out to meet her and helped tow the boat in. Then they had another valiant struggle drawing it up onto the sand. But this time Mary drove a stake deep in the beach, a long way out of reach of the water, and anchored the boat securely with a piece of rope.

"Well, that's that," said Mary, blinking back tears of relief, "and we're all safe."

"Oh, Mary," said Jean, "I've learned more about tides today than I ever learned in school."

"I guess that isn't the last thing this island will teach us, either. Now you dry Blue, and keep an eye on the others, while I see what I can do to dry myself."

"Just one darn thing after another," said Jean, and Mary was still so much excited that she forgot to remind Jean that she should never say "darn."

CHAPTER SIX

The Tepee

"WELL," said Mary the next morning, "we can't count on living in our cave, now that we know about tides."

"You mean it will fill up with water at high tide?"

"I'm afraid so."

"No wonder it looked clammy! If we were only mermaids, it would be just the thing."

"Well, we aren't," said practical Mary. "We've got to discover something else."

They put all the babies in the boat, took off their shoes and stockings, tucked up their skirts, and started off along the beach, Mary wading in front and pulling the boat, Jean coming behind to push and steer. They had decided never to leave the babies alone again.

"This is a wautomobile, Mary," called Jean from the stern.

"A what?"

"Water automobile. Don't you see?—wautomobile."

It was rather hard going sometimes, but a breeze from the land helped to combat the force of the waves and

62

keep the boat offshore. The babies enjoyed the adventure hugely, the twins shouting "Gee-gee!" to Mary to make her go faster, while Ann Elizabeth played peekaboo through her fingers with Jean. At one place where palm trees grew near the shore, they found a cocoanut floating in the water and gladly took it into the boat. About noon they reached their cave. As Mary had expected they found fresh seaweed on the damp floor, and the tracks which they had left the day before had all been washed away.

"It's just too bad," she mourned. "But let's eat lunch, and then go on farther. Surely we'll find a place before night."

The addition of the cocoanut to their rather scanty luncheon put them all in good spirits, and soon they were on their way again.

It was not easy work managing the heavy lifeboat so near the beach. Their arms ached and their bare feet were cut and bruised. But, as Mary often said, a Wallace would not give up in face of difficulties, and in the middle of a hot afternoon their courage was suddenly rewarded. They were thirsty, and the water in the jug, besides being too precious to use freely, was warm and stale.

They had been going along at the same gait for some time, when suddenly Mary stopped and cocked her head to listen. Above the steady pound of waves on sand to which

63

BABY ISLAND

their ears had grown accustomed, was another sound—the clear, sharp gurgling of water running and falling over rocks. And there around the next bend it was—a small bright stream of sparkling water. Hastily beaching the boat, the girls ran to taste it. They threw themselves down beside it, and drank with their mouths to the water. Then they sat up with dripping noses and chins.

"It's good!" cried Mary.

"It's not salty!" cried Jean.

"It's cool!" cried both together.

They jumped up, threw their arms about each other, and tried to do a highland fling. After this they took another drink.

"I never knew water could taste so good," cried Jean. "It's better than pink lemonade or malted milk."

"Oh, I'm so glad!" cried Mary, with happy tears running down her cheeks and splashing into the water. "I'm so glad! I'm so glad!"

"Mary, aren't we like the Ancient Mariner or Balboa discovering the Pacific Ocean or something? Shouldn't we take possession of this place in the name of good Queen Bess or Mary Queen of Scots or something?"

"Well—something," agreed Mary uncertainly. "I think it ought to be in the name of the President of the United States, though, really."

64

"Wait until I tie my blue handkerchief to a stick," cried Jean. "Now! I strike this flag into the soil of Baby Island and take possession of this stream and this island in the name of the President of the United States and Mary and Jean Wallace. Amen!"

"You forgot the babies," said Mary reproachfully.

"They're not of age yet—I don't think they ought to be mentioned in important matters."

"Bye-bye!" shouted the twins from the boat. "Ba-ba, bye-bye!"

"They're speaking for themselves," said Mary, smiling. "Let's take them out and give them all drinks."

The finding of the fresh-water stream at once settled where they should live. Of course, they must live somewhere along its banks. Jean went scouting while Mary looked after the babies, and presently Jean returned to report that she had found the very spot. Following her directions, Mary went upstream a short distance until she came to a little open glade. At the back the stream came down in a pleasant waterfall. Many years of falling water had gradually hollowed out this semi-circular valley, which was about the size of a large house and almost surrounded (except on the side toward the sea) by rock walls. It was so green and sheltered, so snug and homelike, that Mary loved it at once. Above the waterfall waved the fronded

65

wilderness of a tropical jungle. But here they were neither in jungle nor on beach, but in a little corner all their own.

Tired as they were, after their long journey pulling the boat, Mary knew that there was much work to be done before dark. She ran back to where Jean waited with the babies. With the help of the tide which was now in, they securely beached the boat beyond the reach of the waves. Then Mary carried Ann Elizabeth and Jean took Jonah, and each led a tottery twin by the hand to the site of their new home.

"Now, I hate to do this," said Mary, "and as soon as we get settled we won't have to, but today we'll have to stake the babies out like goats."

"Not Jonah, surely," protested Jean.

"No, I guess Jonah will stay put, if we make him a nice

66

little bed. But the others would be tumbling into the stream or falling off cliffs or what not, and you and I have work to do."

So, with the rope which they had found in the lifeboat, the three walking and creeping babies were tied up to palm trees. Ann Elizabeth promptly crept around and around her tree until she was completely wound up, and then she sat down amiably to play with her fingers. The twins pranced and bellowed at the ends of their ropes, but Mary, knowing them safe, paid no attention to them and fell to work.

"We'll have a tepee, Jean," she said. "It's the easiest thing we can build, and I know how. Do you remember the one Cousin Alex made us in the back yard two years ago?"

The first things needed were some long poles. Taking the two hatchets, which had also been part of the lifeboat equipment, they started out to get the poles. Jean, whose knack for discovery always stood them in good stead, found a bamboo grove a little farther upstream, and the long poles, which were both light and strong, seemed just the thing to make the framework of the tepee. They had soon cut enough for their use, and, stripping them of leaves, they stuck them in the soft ground in the form of a large circle. Then they tied the tops together with a piece of rope. The canvas sail, eked out with a few palm leaves, made a very good cover for the tepee. Inside they made beds of boughs and leaves, spreading the tarpaulin over all to keep out the dampness from the ground. With the blankets arranged on top in comfortable beds, it looked as if they should have a very agreeable night. They laid a circle of stones beside the stream, and that evening had their first campfire. It was pleasant to have warm food again, even if it was only heated in cans and cups, but more pleasant still, it was, to have a friendly flame to hold back the dark mystery of the tropical night.

Jean and the babies went to sleep early, but Mary sat a long while by the fire, hating to let it go out. This was their first night back from the beach. What lay in the jungle just beyond? They did not know at all. There might be savages or wild beasts there, for all Mary knew. She had not mentioned her fears to Jean, because she did not want to worry her.

"Well," she said to herself at last, "it certainly won't help any for me to worry. Either we'll be devoured or we won't be devoured, and I couldn't do much to save us anyway." Leaving a little fire burning in the ring of stones, she crawled into the crowded tepee to sleep. Pulling off her dress and folding it neatly, Mary hummed a tune under her breath. She hummed, very softly so as not to waken the others, the tune "Scots, Wha' Hae wi' Wallace Bled."

Sometime later Mary awoke with a start. A frightful howling and chattering filled the air. She sat up straight, and it seemed for a moment as if her heart would stop beating altogether. Even Jean was startled out of her dreams and sat up too. The fire had gone out, but a flood of moonlight silvered everything and made the canvas of the tepee look white between the dark bamboo poles. Suddenly there was a swish of palm leaves, and a small black shadow swung itself across the white canvas. Mary gave a frightened gasp. Was it something inside the tent? But, no, Mary's better judgment told her in an instant that something *outside* the tent had swung by close enough to cast a shadow on their walls. As the shadow flashed by, Jean drew in her breath sharply and then let out such a scream that all the babies awoke and began to scream too.

For a moment the chattering and howling outside ceased. There was a pattering of many little feet, several shadows swung across the canvas, and then the chattering sounded farther and farther away. It was as if many little creatures had been put to flight.

"Well, you certainly scared them, whatever they were," said Mary, "but I must say you didn't set a very good example to the babies. Now you can just help me put 'em to sleep again."

A little cuddling, soothing, and singing finally eased the

69

babies off to sleep. But Mary and Jean were too wide awake now to do more than lie still listening. After the howling and chattering, and the crying of the babies, there was deep silence. Then out of this great silence began to come a faint, persistent crying, very pitiful to hear. Something outside the tepee seemed lost and sad and begging for help. The crying went on and on, so mournfully that Mary could scarcely bear it She turned from side to side, trying to close her ears to the hopeless sound. At last she sat up softly and pulled on her dress.

"You're not going out there, Mary?" begged Jean.

"I've got to go," said Mary. "There's a baby crying."

"Oh, babies!" said Jean, and it seemed to her that for once in her life she'd had enough of them.

Mary slipped out of the tent, and Jean could hear her tiptoeing around and making soft calling noises. Then everything was still for a long time, or so it seemed to Jean.

But at last Mary came softly back, and clinging to the front of her dress was a very tiny monkey. When the girls looked at him he covered his eyes with his little hands and shivered with fright. Mary held him gently, making soft, reassuring noises, and presently he hid himself under her arm, clinging closely to her warm body.

"You see," she said, "the other monkeys ran off and left him. Jeannie, we've got to take in another baby!"

CHAPTER SEVEN

Mary Mixes the Twins

THE next day they put the little monkey out where his mother could find him if she chose, but she never returned for him. The screams from the tepee had frightened the monkeys so that they never wished to return. But it seemed to make very little difference to the baby monkey. He had found a new family which he liked quite as well as the old. The girls fed him and petted him.

Although Mary had been the one to rescue him, he soon became Jean's particular baby. Some spirit of mischief and adventure in the two linked them together almost from the start. Jean named him Prince Charley after the ranch her father managed in Australia, and it was not long before he knew his name and came when he was called. Unfortunately he often got himself into trouble with Mary, because he liked to steal Jonah's bottle, pull Ann Elizabeth's hair, or get the twins into mischief. But he was so gay and amusing that they could forgive him a great deal.

The girls soon settled down to a regular routine of housekeeping. As the days passed Mary checked them off on

71

her calendar, so that they would know where they were in point of time, and Jean as regularly "mailed" her letter to Aunt Emma, sealing it in an empty can and tossing it out to sea. Sometimes the waves brought it back, sometimes on a calm day when the tide was going out it danced away in the sunshine until it was lost to sight. Mary always sighed and shook her head when Jean performed this rite; but she said nothing, as Jean seemed to derive some comfort from it.

One of the first things they had to do was to build a pen for the babies, so that they could play safely without straying away. In the shade of a couple of palms they built a small stockade by driving sharpened sticks close together

into the ground. It was a hard task but well worth the trouble, for the twins and Ann Elizabeth were content to play there for hours without danger.

Another great achievement was the building of the "pram" —perambulator for long, pram for short. This, like the tepee, was an idea which they had got from Cousin Alex's fund of Indian lore. They made a litter of boughs, tied together with the strong sinewy vines that abounded everywhere and some pieces of their precious rope. More vines and rope made a sort of double harness which the girls put around their shoulders. When they wanted to go anywhere, they loaded the litter with blankets and babies and dragged the whole thing along behind them. True, it was very slow, and they once lost Blue off altogether and had to go back nearly a quarter of a mile for him. But on the whole the pram was very successful. They found the abundance of vines useful for many purposes. Jean discovered a natural swing hanging between two trees in the edge of the jungle.

"Don't you let either of them fall, Jean," warned Mary. "I've got an awful responsibility to Mrs. Snodgrass, and I don't know whether she would approve of swinging or not."

"Oh, they love it, Mary, and I'll be awfully careful of them. You know," Jean added a little wistfully, "I'm really beginning to feel settled—now that we have a swing."

They soon discovered that, when the tide was out, the

little sun-warmed pools among the rocks made splendid bathtubs for the babies. One morning while baths were in progress, Jean suddenly began to rub her eyes.

"Mary, do you see what I see?"

"I see four darling babies, if that's what you mean," said Mary happily.

"No, look down at that sandy stretch! Look! There are funny little squirts of water coming up."

"Sure enough," said Mary.

"But Mary, you're so calm about it. I think it's mighty queer to see water squirting right out of the sand. Come on, Pink, you're dry enough, now. Let's investigate." Taking Elisha by the hand, and Prince Charley on her shoulder, she went down the beach to look at the queer little holes from which the water came. She picked up a piece of driftwood, and began to dig where the tiny spout of water had been. Presently she was digging faster and faster.

"Ach! Mary! There's something down here," she called. "And it's going down just as fast as I can dig. Oh, wait a minute, *you!* I'm getting it!" Suddenly she gave a triumphant shout. "Mary, look what the cat brought in!" And Jean held aloft an oval shell.

"Why, Jeannie, it's a clam!" cried Mary. "Aren't you a smart girl! Folks stew them or steam them or something and eat them for dinner."

74

Jean was through with baby washing for the rest of the morning. She ran for the pail, put her clam safely inside it, and began to dig wherever she saw a spout of water. The Pink Twin waddled joyfully behind her, digging very busily, too, but never catching any clams.

> *"Clams! clams!"* [sang Jean].
> *"We haven't got pork chops,*
> *We haven't got hams,*
> *We haven't got mutton*
> *Or beef or lambs;*
> *But we've got clams*
> *An' clams an' clams!"*

The bottom of her pail was well covered when the Pink Twin suddenly uttered a fearful howl.

75

"Murder!" said Jean. "What is it, my pet?"

His voice rose in a series of piercing shrieks. Jean left her pail and ran to his assistance. He sat in a puddle and pointed dramatically to his toe. Jean's anxious eyes saw a small green crab hanging on to his toe for dear life.

"Oh, it's a *crab!*" she cried. "Poor baby, Jean will take it off. Go away, *naughty crab!*" She unloosed the sharp pincers, and the queer little creature skuttled sideways under a rock. Pink stopped crying. Then he pointed to the spot where it had disappeared and said, "Cwab!" Jean was delighted. She picked him up and ran to Mary.

"Pink has learned a new word. Think of it, Mary. He can say 'Crab!' Say 'Crab,' Pink."

But Pink only looked at them. He put up his fingers before his face, he smiled, but he wouldn't say a word.

That noon they had clams for dinner. How good they tasted!

Jean preferred to forage for food and Mary to tend the babies and keep house. So it very often happened that Jean went off alone, returning laden with bananas or cocoanuts or breadfruits, which they didn't know by name but had found delicious when cooked. Sometimes she dug for clams or gathered mussels.

One day she managed to capture a big green crab.

"I'm sure I've heard of people eating cracked crab. I'll

just take him home and crack him up to surprise Mary," she said to herself. "But I'd better not let Elisha see him," she added. "He'd be scared pinker than he is already." So she put the crab inside the pail with a big palm leaf over the top to keep him in. As she came near the tepee, Mary ran out to meet her.

"Oh, Jean, something terrible has happened!"

"Is Prince Charley lost?"

"Oh, no! Worse, Jean."

"Has Jonah swallowed a cocoanut?"

"Oh, no, worse!"

"Well, for pity's sake tell me, Mary."

"I'm trying to, Jean. But you ask questions so fast I can't. Listen! I'll never forgive myself—I've mixed the twins!"

"Mary! Not really!"

"Oh, I don't know how I could have let such a thing happen," wailed Mary. "You see Pink was undressed (I was washing his clothes), and then I went out to see if they were dry and left the twins together. And, when I came back, Blue had managed to wriggle out of his nighty, too, and there they were exactly alike and no way of telling which is which!"

"Shades of Mrs. Snodgrass!" ejaculated Jean solemnly. "Come to Jean, Blue."

Both twins looked up and waved fat hands.

"Pink, come here," begged Jean.

Both babies staggered onto their fat legs and toddled over.

"Elisha! Elijah!"

Both of them answered to either name. It seemed hopeless.

"Well," remarked Jean, "I never did think it made much difference anyway."

Mary, so brave in face of danger, suddenly burst into tears. "You know how I feel about that, Jean," she sobbed. "Each baby has a right to his own name and his own color. I can't help thinking how their mother would feel!"

Ann Elizabeth was creeping about the tent on a tour of inspection. She came to the pail Jean had left in the doorway. She tipped it over gently and took off the palm leaf.

"Pitty," she said. "Pitty."

But no one heard her, for Mary and Jean were too busy trying to identify the twins to heed another baby's prattle.

"Ooh!" said Ann Elizabeth, as the fat green crab walked out of the pail and into the tent. "Ooh! Ooh!"

Still nobody paid any attention. Mary and Jean were just giving up in despair, when suddenly the eyes of one of the twins went wide with terror.

"Cwab!" he shrieked.

Mary and Jean followed his gaze, and there was the fat green crab in the middle of the floor.

"It's Pink!" cried Jean, catching him up to hug him. "Dry your tears, Mary, he's solved his own riddle!"

And so he had.

So the weeks passed, and, as nothing disagreeable happened to them, they began to feel quite at home in the tepee. Now that they had found fresh water and plentiful supplies of fruit and shellfish, Mary had only one great worry. How long would the canned-milk supply hold out? It was worrying her one Saturday morning. She had just been looking at the calendar and thinking that, since tomorrow was Sunday, they might treat themselves to a can of beef, when she noticed how few cans of milk were left. She heaved a deep sigh. It was often difficult being mother to so many. Even Jean needed watching over. Her twenty-third Psalm was getting very rusty from being in a heathen country so long, and Mary resolved that she should say it tomorrow at Sunday worship.

She had Sunday on her mind and she was particularly surprised when Jean burst in, crying, "Friday! Friday!"

"No, dear, it's Saturday," corrected Mary absently. Then something in Jean's tone made her pause.

Jean was panting so that she could scarcely speak.

"Why, what's the matter?" asked Mary.

"I told you—it's Friday. I saw his tracks!"

"You saw whose tracks?" cried Mary.

79

"Oh, Mary, like Robinson Crusoe. Don't you remember? There were tracks in the sand! I saw them!"

"Jean," said Mary, "You're all excited. I'll bet you saw your own tracks and got scared. There is certainly no man Friday around here."

"Oh, isn't there?" cried Jean bitterly. "I guess I'm smart enough to know my own tracks from those of a big savitch!"

"Did you see anything besides tracks?" asked Mary.

"Goodness, Mary! How much do you expect for a nickel? I tell you I saw tracks as big as—as big as—oh, enormstrous! And *one toe was missing!*"

Mary was much troubled. Suppose there really were other people on the island? Would they be unfriendly? "Where did you see the tracks, Jean?"

"Way down the beach—farther than we ever went before. I ran all the way home. Come and I'll show you."

Wide-eyed and pale, Mary followed Jean up the beach.

"There!" panted Jean at last.

Clear and fresh in the moist sand near the water's edge were the tracks of naked feet. No one could possibly imagine them to be Jean's. Farther up they were lost in the loose sand and rocks. They were very large, and the imprint of the middle toe was missing from the left foot.

CHAPTER EIGHT—————————

Hunting Friday

FOR two days, after they had seen the footprints, the children stayed in the tepee. They went out only for such necessities as food and water, and took turns keeping watch at night. They no longer dared light a fire for fear the smoke would lead those big bare feet in their direction.

"I'm sure it's a pirate, Mary," said Jean. "They always have something missing. Mostly it's legs, but why not toes?"

"I'm afraid it's a savage," said Mary. "I only hope it's not the kind who eats babies."

"Oh, Mary!" wailed Jean.

"Well," said brave Mary, "we must face the worst. But I'll fight to the last for my babies. He'll never stew a Snodgrass or an Arlington while Mary Wallace lives and breathes!"

"Same here!" cried Jean, and she began to chant:

> *"Now's the day an' now's the hour.*
> *See the front of battle lour."*

But as time went on and nothing happened, existence grew unbearably dull. The babies were restless, and kept upsetting

81

things and getting into mischief. Prince Charley made a nuisance of himself.

On the evening of the second day in the tepee Jean cried: "Ho-hum! I'd rather be stewed than live like this! If the savitch won't hunt us, let's go and hunt him!"

"Well, Jean, I know how you feel," said Mary. "Of course, it won't do to go and hunt him. But we might as well live comfortably until he finds us."

"No," insisted Jean. "I think we ought to find him. It's like being afraid of ghosts. We'll never feel happy till we know who made those footprints."

"But what shall we do with the babies?"

"We'll take 'em with us. Friday was good to Robinson Crusoe. Maybe our savitch will be good to us."

"Not likely," said Mary, gloomy but wavering, "and don't keep calling him a 'savitch,' please."

"If he wants food," continued Jean, "I'll let him eat me first. My bones will stick in his throat and choke him before he ever gets around to your nice fat ones."

Mary was very doubtful, and yet anything seemed better than sitting in the tent and waiting. "Perhaps a sight of the babies will soften his heart," she said. "It's wonderful what the sight of a sweet, clean baby will do to a hard and cruel heart!"

They agreed that the island needed exploring anyway, for

who knew what dangers or delights lay on the other side?

"We'd better take food enough for several days," said practical Mary. "You know how slowly we travel with the pram."

Jean agreed and helped tie up the cans of beef and milk. "Why, Mary, the milk's nearly gone!" she exclaimed.

"I know," said Mary with tears in her eyes. "I haven't spoken about it, because—well, what can we do? But I don't know how the babies are going to get along on straight cocoanut milk, when this is gone."

They started at daybreak the next morning, traveling cautiously and silently, at least as far as the hilarious twins could be hushed into silence. It was very slow and difficult with the unwieldy pram to pull, and babies always tumbling off when they went over bumps. Nevertheless, by late afternoon, they were in new territory, a part of the island they had never seen before. It looked wilder and more rugged here. But they intended to keep going until they had encircled the island and come back to their own camp once more.

The tide had washed out Friday's tracks, and, although they were continually on the watch, they saw no more. They began to wonder if the tracks had been only a dream, when suddenly Jean cried, *"Look!"* It was a very small thing—a tag of blue cloth caught on a thornbush. But they were both on the alert at once.

"It's a piece of blue shirt," said Mary positively.

"Then he's not a savitch—he's a pirate!" hissed Jean.

"He might still be a savage," said Mary staunchly. "Mr. and Mrs. Snodgrass were taking trunks full of shirts to put on the savages. They said they were going to clothe them in righteousness, but I think it was mostly blue shirts. It's a very good sign. He probably won't be so wild."

"Remember that missing toe, Mary. That looks pretty wild to me!"

"Well, we must go very carefully now. He may not be far away."

The ground had been growing rougher, and soon it led up to some rocky cliffs by the sea. They began to discern faint traces of a path leading to the top. With some difficulty they dragged the delighted babies up after them, and paused at the top with open mouths. Below them spread a beautiful little harbor with crescent-shaped beach and white sand. And at one side was a little *house!* Oh, a very tiny house made of driftwood and bark and pieces of tin, but after all a house. The path was more clearly marked, going down the cliff, and led to the very door of the house. The girls stood spellbound, gazing at this entrancing sight. Even the babies seemed touched with awe and looked with round eyes of surprise at the house on Baby Island.

Everything was silent around the little house. A few sea gulls flying over the harbor were the only signs of life.

"Let's scout," said Jean at last.

Each took a baby on her arm and a twin by the hand and began to scout. This meant slipping behind rocks and brush, and gradually working their way down without being seen. It might have been impossible, had the twins not caught the spirit of the game and behaved like good Indians. Soon they reached the bottom of the cliff and squatted behind a clump of bushes to look at the house.

"Isn't it bee-autiful?" sighed Jean.

Mary's eyes were full of tears.

"Well, it isn't exactly beautiful," she said, "but it kind of reminds me of home."

Suddenly the Blue Twin broke away from Jean and went staggering out after a yellow butterfly. Jean sprang after him, and the others followed in terrified silence. Around the corner of the shanty, they all stopped in amazement. Even Blue stood still and gazed. Stretched in a hammock, softly snoring, lay Friday! He was not a savage, so he must be a pirate. He wore a blue shirt and tattered duck pants.

"The toe!" breathed Mary. Sure enough, his feet were bare and the middle toe on his left foot was missing. He had a very large nose, and his slightly open mouth was surrounded by a strong, black beard.

"It's him," whispered Jean, and Mary was too astonished at the moment to tell her to say "It's he."

How long they stood and gazed they never could have said, but suddenly there was a little rustling noise inside the shanty, and a very hoarse voice began singing:

> *"Oh, Bedelia,*
> *I'd like to steal yuh!"*

Jean's nerves were not very steady by this time, and she couldn't help screaming. The pirate sat up as if he had been shot. He rubbed his eyes and looked at them. Two girls and four babies stared at him with six pairs of fascinated eyes. An expression of the liveliest surprise crossed his face. Then he went white with terror, jumped out of the hammock, and hurled himself into the shanty, slamming the door behind him.

"Now see what you've done, Jean," said Mary severely. "When you feel one of those screams coming, you ought to hold it in."

"That awful voice!" gasped Jean. As she spoke they heard it again.

> *"Oh, Bedelia,*
> *I'd like to—"*

"Shut yer trap, Halfred," growled the voice of the pirate.

There was silence. Then they could see one eye and a bit

86

of the pirate's beard as he peeped at them through his little window.

Mary's usual bravery in case of emergencies came to her rescue now. It seemed to her that both Jean and the stranger were behaving very stupidly. They had come down the hill expecting to be afraid of the pirate, and here he was being afraid of them. She went up and knocked at the door.

"We won't hurt you," she said, "if you won't hurt us. We have just dropped in to call."

"Oh, Mary," whispered Jean. "There's someone else in there, too. Didn't you hear that awful voice?"

But Mary was unmoved. She knocked again. "I know you weren't expecting us," she said, "but you might at least say 'How do you do.' We are your neighbors, and we are awfully glad that you are not a savage."

The door opened a few inches at a time, and the pallid pirate looked out.

"You're not very brave, are you?" remarked Mary kindly.

"Are ye real?" asked the pirate in a hoarse whisper.

"Of course!" said Mary. "What did you think? We're going to Australia, but our ship got wrecked, so we're stopping here on the way."

"*Young 'uns!*" exclaimed the man in a dazed fashion, "and I came 'ere to be free from young 'uns!" He sat down on the doorstep and held his head.

"How did you get here?" asked Mary.

"This 'ere is my 'ome," said the pirate. "I come 'ere to get peace."

"Pieces of eight," suggested Jean, whose fear was now lost in curiosity. "I knew he was a pirate."

"Pirate?" said the man crossly. "Pirate be blowed! I'm a honest Henglish seaman, I ham."

"There's something wrong with his speech," said Jean. "Can you understand him?"

"What is your name?" asked Mary politely.

"Well, mum, 'tis 'Arvey Peterkin, if it does ye any good to know."

"'Arvey," repeated Jean. "I never heard that name before."

"He means Harvey," explained Mary. "He's mixed up on his aitches. Were you shipwrecked, too, Mr. Peterkin?"

"Did you build this house yourself?" asked Jean. "How long have you been here?"

"Do boats ever stop here?"

"Where do you get your milk?"

The unfortunate English seaman put his hands over his ears.

"Questions!" he cried, "just like my brother's wife, Maggie! *Young 'uns!* Just like my brother's wife, Maggie! I come 'ere to be rid o' that."

"I'm sorry," said Mary politely, "but there are so many things we want to know."

"Bly'me!" went on Mr. Peterkin bitterly. "I never thought to see babies on a desert hi'land. No, sir! I give up my 'ome, I give up my sweetheart, Belinda, I give up all I 'olds dear, to get free from the likes o' you! But 'ere you be, aknocking on my werry door!"

"Oh!" said Mary and Jean, rather taken aback, and Mary added regretfully, "You aren't very glad to see us, are you?"

"You asks your questions so fast, maybe I am an' maybe I'm not. Give me time to think it over."

"You see we haven't had a chance to ask questions for a very long time. I expect that's why we ask so many."

"It muddles me," said Mr. Peterkin plaintively.

Just then a frightful uproar broke out in the cabin. Prince Charley, unnoticed by the girls, had gone inside to explore, and they could now hear his angry chatter mingled with outraged cries from the hoarse voice which had previously been heard singing.

"Oh, save my Charley from the pirates!" screamed Jean.

" 'Ey Halfred, what's the matter?" shouted Mr. Peterkin, going inside.

There was a moment's pause, full of terrible suspense. Then Prince Charley came out first, triumphantly clutching in his small brown hand several long green and red feathers. Next came Mr. Peterkin, very angry, with a large red and green parrot on his shoulder, ruffling its feathers and crying hoarsely: "Oh, you would, would you? Oh, you would, would you?"

Jean, with Charley on her shoulder, and Mr. Peterkin, with Halfred on his, gazed at each other angrily.

See the front of battle lour!

But just at this moment Mary saw something which made her forget everything else. Around the shanty had come a little white goat. She uttered only one word, but that one word meant everything to Mary.

"Milk!"

90

CHAPTER NINE

Another Baby

"**A** GOAT!" cried Mary. "Goats give milk! The babies shall be fed!"

Even Jean forgot Prince Charley's troubles in contemplating the marvel of a goat.

"Keep away from them goats, *if* you please!" shouted Mr. Peterkin angrily. But he had spoken too late. Mary never saw a little animal without loving it, and her affection was always returned. She and the little white goat were already making friends. Two other goats followed the first one, and in a moment Mary was surrounded by them, and was busy making soft, baby-talk noises to them and scratching their foreheads between their horns. "It's just here that you scratch them," she said tenderly, "and how they love it!"

"Oh, look, Mary," said Jean, laying Jonah in the "pirate's" hammock and hurrying forward. "There's a baby one, too. But there's something wrong with it. Look how thin it is."

Indeed, the tiny kid, which wobbled along behind the others was a pitiable sight. When it came too near the older goats, they turned and pushed it away with their horns.

"Why, Mr. Peterkin!" cried Mary. "This baby goat is starving!"

"You tellin' me?" said Mr. Peterkin crossly. "Don't I know that?"

"Well, why don't you do something about it?" asked Mary.

"Bly'me," shouted Mr. Peterkin, " 'E won't eat, th' little beggar. 'Is Ma died last week an' 'e won't eat nothin', an' them big goats, they won't let the little beggar come near them, they won't. Hunnatural, I calls it, hunnatural!"

"Have you got a bottle?" asked Mary. "I'll get him to eat."

"Meddlesome young 'uns," grumbled Mr. Peterkin, "meddlesome, I calls 'em." But just the same he fetched an empty rum bottle and warmed some goats' milk in a pan.

Mary made a hole in the cork of the bottle, so that a small amount of the milk could come through, and when the bottle was filled she stuck the cork in tightly.

"Jonah's bottle would be better," she said, "but Mrs. Snodgrass was always so careful about sterilizing things, I guess she wouldn't want a goat using it."

" 'E won't eat," said Mr. Peterkin pessimistically. "Ye're wastin' your time."

But Mary knew better. She took the little goat on her lap, stroking him and talking kindly to him. At first he

92

turned away his head and refused to take the bottle. But Mary did not give up trying, and, when at last she succeeded in getting it into his mouth and he tasted the warm milk, he greedily drank it and bleated for more.

"Strike me pink!" said Mr. Peterkin in surprise, and for the first time since they had met him, he looked really pleased.

"Now," said Mary, when the baby goat had had his fill, "we've come about as far as we can today, Mr. Peterkin, and I'm afraid you'll have to let us spend the night."

"Not if I can 'elp it!" cried Mr. Peterkin, the frightened look returning to his face. "Me an' Halfred an' the goats, we live here *alone.*"

"We won't be any bother," said Mary. "We have our own food and camping things. If you'll just give us a little milk for the babies' supper, we'll go 'way up your beach and not bother you at all."

Mr. Peterkin looked very glum. "See 'ere," he said. "My brother 'Enry 'e made a great mistake. 'E went an' got married, 'e did; a awful naggin' woman 'e married, name of Maggie. An' they have twelve young 'uns, awful meddlesome young 'uns. I was promised to be married myself to a lady named Belinda, as fair a wench as ever balanced a tray. But, sez I, 'twill be 'Enry an' Maggie all over, sez I. So I hups an' runs away to this 'ere hi'land to be rid of young 'uns for the rest of my life. That's why ye're not welcome, d'ye see?"

"Yes, I see," said Mary. "You told us that before. You are very, very much mistaken about young ones, Mr. Peterkin. If you knew us better, I am sure that you would like us. But we promise to go away first thing in the morning. Now, please do be a good man and give us some goats' milk for supper, and we won't bother you another bit."

Grumbling a great deal, Mr. Peterkin filled their pail half full of goats' milk.

94

"My, you certainly have a lot!" said Jean admiringly. "What do you do with all of it?"

"Cheese," said Mr. Peterkin glumly.

"But you surely can't eat so much cheese all by yourself, can you?"

"Questions! questions! questions!" grumbled the honest seaman, and at a sign from Mary, Jean wisely held her tongue.

The pram made a very good bed with the blankets spread over it, and it was quite pleasant sleeping once again under the bright stars.

They made a campfire and roasted bananas and steamed clams, which smelled very good in the clear night air, and tasted even better. And the babies smacked their lips over the fresh goats' milk.

The baby goat had gone with them to their camp and followed Mary's every move, bleating piteously. This seemed to anger Mr. Peterkin still more, and he came down and got it and shut it roughly into his goat pen.

"My goodness!" said Jean, "I almost b'lieve I'd rather have found a pirate or a savitch than that old crosspatch."

"Oh, *no*, Jean," said Mary. "I feel so sorry for him. Not to like babies! Think what he's missing! Besides, if he had been a savage he might have eaten us, and a pirate might have made us walk the plank. Mr. Peterkin just wants us

95

to go away. And then he owns goats! Somehow, Jean, we've got to persuade him to let us have milk!"

"But how?" asked Jean. "He's about as sociable as a sour oyster."

"We'll have to work on his better feelings, of course."

"Do you think he has any?"

"Oh, Jean, everybody has better feelings if you can just get at them."

"I think Mr. Peterkin's are pretty far under," said Jean gloomily.

"You leave him to me," said Mary.

They were awakened in the morning by a hoarse voice singing:

> *"Oh, Bedelia,*
> *I'd like to steal yuh!"*

Halfred, the parrot, had come over to inspect camp. He walked around and around them while Jean held the chattering Charley safely in her arms.

"Good morning, Halfred," said Mary politely. "I hope that you had a good night."

"Oh, you would, would you? Oh, you would, would you?" said Halfred sarcastically.

Mary held out a small piece of hardtack. Halfred took it in one claw and, standing one-legged, nibbled it daintily, cocking his yellow eye at them the while.

"Well, bless my soul!" he remarked. "Well, bless my soul and body!"

Mary held out another bit of hardtack.

"Oh, you would, would you?" said Halfred, but this time his tone had lost its sarcasm and was quite ingratiating. Presently he was like one of the family, letting the twins pet him and call him "Birdie," and Mary scratch his head and smooth his tail feathers. For Mary knew the right place to scratch parrots' heads, too.

In the midst of this pleasant domestic scene, Mr. Peterkin arrived like a thundercloud.

"Halfred, come out o' that!" he commanded sternly.

Halfred flew obediently to his master's shoulder, tweaking his ear and remarking hoarsely, "Man the pumps, Captain, man the pumps!"

"Look 'ere," said Mr. Peterkin, addressing Mary, "that kid's sick again. 'E won't eat no'ow. I gives 'im the bottle just like you did, an' bly'me if 'e don't shun me cold."

"Well," said Mary, "of course he won't take the bottle if you're cross with him. You have to make yourself look and sound like his mother."

"Me?" roared Mr. Peterkin. "Me look an' sound like a nanny goat?"

"That's what I said."

"Look 'ere, Miss. You come give 'im the bottle. I'll give

ye milk for yer young 'uns' breakfast, if ye'll get the little beggar to take 'is."

Mary wanted nothing better. "Here, you hold these babies for me," she said, putting Jonah and Ann Elizabeth into the astonished seaman's arms, and she ran off to the goat pen.

Jean followed her, holding the twins by the hand, with Halfred and Charley hopping along on each side. Last of all came the dazed Mr. Peterkin, carrying the two babies as gingerly as if they had smallpox. Ann Elizabeth gave Mr. Peterkin a long look, and then her face dimpled into a lovely baby smile.

"Pitty," said Ann Elizabeth, touching his fierce black whiskers. "Pitty-pitty."

Mr. Peterkin was embarrassed, but he was also just a little flattered. Nobody had ever before called his beard pretty.

It took Mary only a moment to persuade the baby goat to take his breakfast. All he wanted was a kind hand and a gentle voice to administer it. When he had finished it, Mary turned to Mr. Peterkin.

"Now, I'll show you how to get his confidence," she said, and in a moment the haughty Mr. Peterkin was taking lessons in the art of looking and sounding like a mama nanny goat.

"Well, blow me down!" he remarked hoarsely, when Mary told him that he had done well at his lesson.

Meanwhile inquisitive Jean and the twins were exploring Mr. Peterkin's shanty.

"Oh, Mary," cried Jean, from the shanty door, "he's got a phonograph."

As it happened, the phonograph was Mr. Peterkin's greatest weakness, and now he couldn't resist showing it off. Making a great pretense of grumbling, he went into the shanty and wound it up. It was an old-fashioned affair with a large horn shaped like a purple morning-glory. The records were little black-wax cylinders. With a certain amount of pride and condescension, Mr. Peterkin played two records for them: "In the Shade of the Old Apple Tree," and "Oh, Bedelia." Halfred, perching himself upon the horn, sang the choruses. He was quite off key and about a measure behind, but nobody minded that.

"So that's where he learned it," said Mary, "and nearly scared Jean to death!"

Jean and the babies were delighted, but soon tidy Mary could do nothing but gaze about the awful disarray of Mr. Peterkin's one room.

"Oh, Mr. Peterkin!" she said, "what a dreadful mess!"

"I'm not a 'ousekeeper, Miss," said he, apologetically.

"I should say not!"

"Oh, but it's a lovely mess, Mary!" cried Jean. "What with the phonograph and *Pharaoh's Horses* in that great gold picture frame, and the shells and ship models, and the iron stove, and that great brass-bound chest. What's in that, Mr. Peterkin?"

"I say, you leave that chest alone, you 'ear?" Mr. Peterkin was angry again, and Jean retreated rapidly. "You're not to touch that, *never!* D'you 'ear?"

"But his bed's not made," said Mary, unable to think of anything else, "and the dust is terrible."

"Well, I 'ates 'ousework!" cried Mr. Peterkin crossly. " 'Tis the only 'ardship in living by myself. Cookin' is 'ateful, too, but a man's got to live even on a desert hi'land!"

Suddenly Mary's eyes grew starry with an idea.

"Look here!" she said. "If one of us came over every week and cleaned your house and cooked up some food for you, would you give us milk for the babies? Would you?"

He scratched his head. "You'd bother me," he growled.

"No, we promise not to bother! We'll cross our hearts, won't we, Jean?"

Solemnly they crossed their hearts.

"Women!" snorted Mr. Peterkin. "Babies! I thought I'd escaped them."

"Oh, come, come!" said Mary sensibly. "You're being awfully silly, you know. We won't hurt you at all, and we're offering to take all your troublesome housework off your hands. Think how nice it would be to have a tidy cabin and some well-cooked food while you go out hunting or lie in your hammock, and all we ask is a little milk for the babies. You have a lot more milk than you need yourself."

Mr. Peterkin looked at her and scratched his head. He looked at Jean and at each of the babies. When he looked at Ann Elizabeth, she burst into smiles and said, "Pitty-pitty." Mr. Peterkin actually blushed. Then he turned to Halfred.

"What say, Halfred?" he asked doubtfully. Halfred flew onto his shoulder and tweaked his ear.

"Man the pumps, Captain, man the pumps!" he remarked genially.

"Well," said Mr. Peterkin. "We'll give 'er a try. But be'ave yourselves! That's all I say. Be'ave yourselves! An' never for *no* reason look into that chest o' mine!"

CHAPTER TEN

Mr. Peterkin's Toe

So Baby Island was not a desert island any longer, with Mr. Peterkin and Halfred and the goats living just around the other side. There was even a boat, Mr. Peterkin told them, which called at the island every two years to leave Mr. Peterkin's supplies and a letter from Belinda.

"Oh, how soon will it come?" cried Mary.

"Just left, Miss, about two months gone."

"Two years to wait!" said Mary sadly, and Jean cried, "Oh, Mary, they will have forgotten all about us in two years!"

So the girls went back to the tepee—a little happy and a little sad.

Every Wednesday morning at daybreak either Mary or Jean started off to clean Mr. Peterkin's house, while the other stayed at the tepee with the babies. When Mary went, Mr. Peterkin's house was shining clean and he had a nice pan of biscuits or a cocoanut pudding. He had a bounteous store of supplies on his shelves, so that cooking should have been easy. But when Jean went, things did not always shine

so brightly, and instead of golden biscuits there was a
fallen cake or what Jean called a "flumperty-wumperty,"
which was a mixture of whatever she could find in Mr.
Peterkin's cupboard. However, on Jean's days there was
certainly more fun, for the phonograph played most of the
time and Halfred sang and Charley danced or swung from
the rafters by his tail. On these occasions poor Mr. Peterkin, unable to bear "young 'uns," went into the jungle to
hunt, or far up the beach for gulls' eggs. There was only
one thing which spoiled Jean's visits for her. Mr. Peterkin
had forbidden her to look into his chest.

"It's that chest of his that worries me, Mary," remarked
Jean one evening after she had been at the shanty. "Think
of having to see it there every time I go, and not knowing
what's inside it."

"Oh, old sailors always have sea chests, Jean."

"So do pirates, Mary, and theirs are full of poltroons."

"Don't you mean doubloons, dear?"

"Well, anyway, I can't rest until I know."

"Jean, you know that story we had in our reader about
Pandora? She was just the kind of girl you are and couldn't
rest until she knew what was inside everything."

"I don't think I ever read that story," said Jean uncom-
fortably.

"Then I'll tell you. She finally opened the chest to see

103

what it held, and all the troubles and sicknesses and fearful things in the world that had been shut up in there flew out and went to work again."

"Well, I never said I was going to look, did I?" demanded Jean.

"No, of course not," said Mary. "I just thought maybe you ought to know about Pandora."

"Yes, and there was that awful thing that happened to Bluebeard's wife, too, wasn't there, Mary?"

"Yes, Bluebeard had definitely told her not to look, and she went and did. It served her right to find all those ladies hanging by their hair."

"It certainly did!" agreed Jean heartily. "But you wouldn't call Mr. Peterkin's whisker exactly blue, would you, Mary? Or would you?"

"It's very, very black," said Mary. "Sometimes very black things are almost blue."

Jean shuddered. "Of course, I'm not really interested in his old chest," she said. "But what I do want to know is how he lost his toe. There must be a good story about that. I wish you'd ask him, Mary."

"Why don't you?"

"Maybe I will sometime, if I feel quite brave."

Mr. Peterkin was harsh, but he never forgot to pay them with a pail of goats' milk. The girls had learned to heat it on Mr. Peterkin's stove, so that it would not sour quickly, and, by keeping it in the cold stream which flowed past the tepee, they were able to have sweet milk for the babies for nearly a week. Toward the end of the week, however, they had to fall back on canned milk, and Mary began to wonder how they could get the fresh goats' milk more often. It was certainly a long way around to Mr. Peterkin's house, and, even without the babies, it took them several hours to walk each way, besides doing Mr. Peterkin's work.

"But we can't move any nearer because of leaving our stream," said Mary. "Of course, Mr. Peterkin has a spring at his place, but he'd never let us live beside him, and I'm not sure I'd want to either."

"If we could go through the jungle," said Jean, "it would be nearer."

"I know," said Mary, "but we'd be sure to get lost."

"Mr. Peterkin has never been over here," said Jean. "Maybe he doesn't know how far we go every week."

"I expect he doesn't care. But, listen, Jean, why don't we invite him over to dinner sometime? Let's do it on a Sunday when he can come to Sunday school. It might do his bad character a lot of good."

"It might," said Jean doubtfully, "but he's got an awful bad character, and I don't think that me saying the twenty-third Psalm would do anybody much good."

"Well, it certainly does *you* a lot of good, Jean. Besides, we'll sing 'Scots, Wha' Hae wi' Wallace Bled,' and maybe I'll preach a sermon, if I can think of some good ways to reform a character like Mr. Peterkin's. Then we'll give him something good to eat—that always helps to reform people. You hardly ever see anyone acting bad on a full stomach."

But somehow the invitation was always delayed. Mr. Peterkin had a frightful way of scowling that made it very difficult even for Mary to say, "Won't you drop in for a plain family dinner next Sabbath after service?" as Aunt Emma used to say to her friends in Scotsville.

The next time that Jean went around the island to do Mr. Peterkin's cleaning, she resolved to solve at least one of the mysteries surrounding him. Pandora and Mrs. Bluebeard had scared her temporarily out of thoughts about his chest, but there was still his toe. She found him taking his ease as usual in the hammock. Halfred flew out to greet her and lit upon her shoulder. Prince Charley was occupying the other shoulder at the moment and they always skirmished cheerily about her ears, Halfred trying to tweak Charley's tail and Charley grabbing a handful of red and green feathers. But on the whole they were very good friends by now. "If only Mr. Peterkin had as nice a disposition as Halfred's," thought Jean. She went and stood before the hammock until Mr. Peterkin lifted the palm-leaf fan off his face and looked at her.

"Well?" he said.

"Mr. Peterkin, how did you lose your toe?"

"I knew that was comin'," cried the unfortunate seaman. "I been lookin' for it all along. Questions! questions! and now this one! 'Ow did I lose me toe? Bly'me, I'll tell ye!"

Jean gave two small pieces of hardtack to Halfred and Charley to keep them quiet and seated herself cross-legged in front of the hammock.

"All right, I'm ready."

" 'Twas one time I was lost in the heart of darkest Hafrica," narrated Mr. Peterkin. "The pygmies was after me—"

"Pig—whats?" asked Jean politely.

"Pygmies, them little men with poisoned harrows," said Mr. Peterkin with unusual patience.

Jean nodded excitedly. This was going to be thrilling.

"One harrow narrowly missed my 'ead as I run through the jungle, and another cut out a piece of my whisker. I run for all I was worth, but them little men was faster. Just behind me they kept, and just out of sight. At last when I seemed to be gainin' on 'em, blow me down! if I didn't come to a roarin' river! 'Ow to get across? They was comin' along be'ind me! They'd 'ave 'ad me in a minute, and the river was full of halligators!"

"How awful!" said Jean, feeling a new tenderness for poor Mr. Peterkin.

"Indeed you may say so," said the brave seaman with satisfaction. "I thought my last hour was upon me. But salvation was at 'and. Just as I reached the bank of the river, I see a great snake with 'is tail coiled round a branch hanging over the river. 'Is 'ead an' neck was 'angin' out about five yards or so, an' 'e was swingin' it back an' forth, rhythmic-like, from one side of the river to the other."

"Like a pendulum?"

"Like a pendulum."

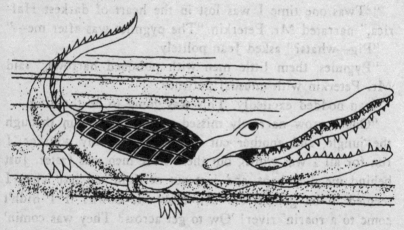

"Oh, Mr. Peterkin, what did you do?"

"When 'e swung back on my side of the river, I caught

'old of 'im an' I gave a mighty jump. Away we went, sailin'
through the air, an' we'd a-fetched up right enough on
tother bank if it hadn't been that the beggar was so slippery.
Slippery 'e were, slippery as a heel. I lost me grip, and
just as we was about to make the bank, I felt myself fallin'.
Down, down, I went, just into the hedge of the river, an'
there a halligator caught me an' bit off me toe as neat as
your granny could do it with her shears. I've always cher-
ished the 'ope that it gave 'im hindigestion."

"But you escaped?" breathed Jean.

"I'm 'ere," said Mr. Peterkin. He closed his eyes, and
began to fan himself softly with the palm leaf.

Jean was kinder to Mr. Peterkin's house that day than
she had been before. She spread the bed so smoothly and
dusted so well, and the cake was neither burned nor fallen!
For surely Mr. Peterkin had a right to tender care after
all that he had been through.

She hurried all the way home to tell Mary, but, when
she arrived, Mary didn't give her a chance.

"Jeannie, dear," said Mary, coming out to meet her, "I'm
an awfully forgetful person. As soon as you had gone this
morning I knew that I had forgotten to tell you something
interesting. The babies just drove it completely out of my
head, but I'm going to tell you right now because you were
so anxious to know and were afraid to ask yourself. It's

about Mr. Peterkin's toe. I asked him the last time I was over."

"He told me today," said Jean with a shade of disappointment.

"Oh, then you know about the Harabs and the sandstorm and the hungry camel?"

Jean's mouth fell open. At last she closed it and said, "No, but I know about the pygmies and the snake and the halligators."

"Oh, no, dear," said Mary gently, "it was like this: Mr. Peterkin was in the desert in Harabia, and a very fierce tribe of Harabs was after him. He was escaping and escaping over the desert sands on his trusty camel when suddenly he saw a dark cloud on the horizon. It came closer and closer, barring his way, and suddenly he saw that it was a terrific sandstorm. The Harabs were galloping, galloping close behind him, but he saw that his only chance to survive was in lying down beside his trusty camel and letting the storm blow over him. Jeannie, that storm lasted for seven days and seven nights. Mr. Peterkin says that camels do not get thirsty for days at a time, but that they do get terribly hungry. His camel was so hungry, before the storm blew over, that Mr. Peterkin was afraid he would take a bite out of him, and one night, while Mr. Peterkin dozed off to sleep—"

"Did what?" asked Jean breathlessly.

"Take a bite out of him. He bit off his toe, said Mr. Peterkin, 'as neat as your granny could do it with her shears.'"

"Mary," said Jean solemnly, "you better get that sermon ready. He's worse than you suppose."

"What do you mean?" asked Mary. "I felt real sorry for him."

"I mean just this," said Jean, "he told me he lost his toe in Hafrica, escaping from the pygmies."

"Maybe," said Mary charitably, "maybe he has two toes missing."

"I never noticed it," Jean remarked grimly, setting her mouth in a firm line. "I guess we'll have to reform him all right, and the sooner we get started the better."

111

CHAPTER ELEVEN

Mary Preaches a Sermon

SO THE girls took their courage in their hands and invited Mr. Peterkin and Halfred over for dinner the very next Sunday. He was quite cross about it and made a great many remarks about "meddlesome young 'uns," but at last he accepted for himself and Halfred.

Jean was all for Psalms and sermons without food, but Mary insisted that food and kindness must form the backbone of any program of reform.

"It's too bad the Snodgrasses aren't here," lamented Jean. "They're so used to reforming savitches, it would be easy for them."

"I'm counting a lot on the babies," said Mary softly. "There's nothing like the sight of some clean, sweet, innocent babies."

"Oh, shucks! You always say that, Mary. It didn't seem to make much difference at Mr. Peterkin's house that day. He just hates babies."

"Nobody really hates babies, Jean. He just thinks he does. We've got to give him a chance."

The girls were busy for several days preparing the feast. By this time they had a tidy collection of dishes made from cocoanut shells, empty cans, flat stones, and large shells picked up on the beach. They made napkins and tablecloths of large leaves, and spoons of small shells, and so they were able to set a dainty table. It was similar to the way in which they had served mud-pie meals in Scotsville, only now they served real food which they had cooked over their own campfire. Jean brought in the finest bananas and breadfruits, the largest crabs and clams, and the best of everything she could find, while Mary used all her skill as a cook to prepare them.

Mr. Peterkin, with Halfred on his shoulder, arrived late. He was quite red in the face from walking so far in the heat, and he was puffing like a steam engine.

"Blow me down!" he exclaimed. "Why did ye build your 'ouse so far around here? 'Tis a fearful tiresome walk on a warm day."

"It certainly is!" said Jean. "We know, because we have to walk over to your house and back every Wednesday."

"But this is why our house stands here," said Mary, holding out a cocoanut shell full of cool fresh water. Mr. Peterkin drained its contents, then he let out a long contented "A-ah!" and wiped his mouth with the back of his hand.

113

"Now you sit right down in the shade and make yourself at home."

Mr. Peterkin obeyed with a heavy sigh. " 'Oo built your 'ouse for you?" he asked.

"We built it ourselves."

"Well, I never!"

"It's not as stylish as yours, but it's quite homelike."

"When do we eat?" next asked Mr. Peterkin.

"Questions! questions!" grumbled Jean with a twinkle in her eye, but Mary replied politely: "Church first. It's Sunday, you know, and I've prepared a sermon."

"Well, tan my hide!" said Mr. Peterkin, too surprised to protest.

"We didn't really plan to tan your hide—" said Mary politely, "only bring you to judgment, if you don't mind. Now if you'll just sit quietly under that palm tree, please. And I'm sure you won't mind holding Jonah and Ann Elizabeth for us, as Jean and I have to be active in the service."

Mr. Peterkin's mouth fell open in the middle of his whiskers, but, before he could reply, he found himself jouncing babies again.

"Pitty-pitty!" said Ann Elizabeth, reaching for Mr. Peterkin's whiskers.

"Now we will please come to order," said Mary, and everybody was quiet.

114

The twins and Prince Charley had learned to sit quietly on large stones which Mary provided for them during Sunday services, and Halfred, being a smart bird, was quick to follow their example.

"Now before we start the service," said Mary firmly, "there's one point that has to be cleared up. Mr. Peterkin, will you kindly tell us how you lost your toe?"

Mr. Peterkin, still too much surprised to have regained his usual bad temper, cleared his throat and swallowed several times so that his Adam's apple bobbed up and down under his whisker.

" 'Twas many years ago when I were a lad in Harabia," he began in a slow voice, which was touched with wistful memories.

"You see, Jean?" cried Mary. "Harabia! You must have misunderstood him."

"Mr. Peterkin!" shouted Jean. "You told me Hafrica and the pygmies!"

Mr. Peterkin looked gently pained. "*I* beg your pardon," he said thoughtfully. " 'Twas in Halbania, the winter of the great snow."

"Halbania!" cried the girls in an outraged chorus.

The honest seaman looked more and more confused.

"No, p'r'aps it weren't Halbania. Haustralia! Haustralia were the spot! 'Twere a dark an' moonless night in the

Haustralian bush, an' bushmen were on my trail. My 'erd
of trusty kangaroos 'ad just stampeded an'—"

"Mr. Peterkin!" cried Mary indignantly. "Be careful what
you say about Australia. Our father lives there, and I know
he hasn't any herds of trusty kangaroos. You're just making
up tales! A wickeder man I never saw!"

"And you an honest seaman!" said Jean reproachfully.

"Pitty-pitty!" said Ann Elizabeth softly, stroking Mr.
Peterkin's black beard.

"Wicked, Miss?" said Mr. Peterkin, with a startled look
in his eyes.

"Yes, wicked!" said Mary firmly. "Why don't you tell the
truth?"

"Look 'ere, Miss," said Mr. Peterkin with tears in his
eyes. "I 'aven't 'ad a very lively sort of life, way out 'ere on
a desert hi'land. If I told you 'ow I really lost my toe,
you'd think it was tame. Tame, that's what it is! Tame! I
'ave to make up these tales to keep my courage up."

"But they ought to hang together," said Jean.

"Now, Mr. Peterkin," said Mary gently. "You'd better
stick to the truth. You know they always say truth is stranger
than fiction."

"Not in my case, Miss."

"Go on and tell us," said Mary. "It will be good for your
soul."

116

Mr. Peterkin covered his face with his hands. "It's drab, that's what it is. Drab!"

"Man the pumps, Captain, man the pumps," remarked Halfred hoarsely.

This seemed to put some courage into the old seaman, for he lifted his head and came out with the truth. "I were 'aying in Hengland," he began.

"What were he doing?" asked Jean in an earnest whisper.

"Haying," whispered Mary. "Don't interrupt him."

"An' I dropped a pitchfork on my toe. 'Twas as simple as that. I dropped a pitchfork on my toe. 'Twere very sharp an' it cut my toe off as neat—as neat—"

"'As neat as your granny could do it with her shears,'" chorused Mary and Jean.

"*That's* the truth at any rate!" said Mr. Peterkin with a great sigh, and he was actually smiling with relief.

"Good!" said Mary. "Now we know, and I'm sure you feel much better, Mr. Peterkin. Now let's sing 'Onward, Christian Soldiers!'"

Mary led off in her clear voice, and Jean joined in. The twins beat time with their hands and made delighted noises. This was better than meat and drink to the gifted parrot, and before they had sung many lines he came bringing up the rear in his hoarse voice. Even Mr. Peterkin, cleansed by his confession, joined in with several lusty "Honwards."

Mary had selected "Thou shalt not bear false witness" as the text of her sermon, but Mr. Peterkin was already so chastened that it seemed a pity to rub it in. So she improvised a very cheery little sermon on a number of texts: "Be ye kind," "Do unto others as you would have others do unto you," "Suffer the little children to come unto me," and "Love thy neighbor as thyself," all of which Mr. Peterkin seemed to need very badly. The last text appeared to Mary most appropriate, and she particularly emphasized the duties of neighbors cast away on desert islands. She hastened the end of it a trifle, because she smelled the bananas, which she had left roasting among the coals, beginning to burn. As she drew her sermon to a hasty close, she thought with pride that it must have benefited Mr. Peterkin very much, but, upon looking more closely at him she discovered that his eyes were closed and that he and the two babies had gone fast asleep.

"Too bad," said Mary, shaking her head, "but I guess it can't be helped. I'll excuse you from your psalm, Jean."

"Whoopee!" said Jean.

"Well," said Mary to herself, as she bustled about serving up dinner, "maybe the sleep and holding the babies did him as much good as a sermon. As I've often said, there's a heap of good in just holding a nice clean baby."

Indeed, something seemed to have improved Mr. Peterkin's disposition, for he was quite agreeable all during dinner, and willingly took second helpings without any urging. He even spoke fondly of Belinda.

"She's still awaitin' for me," he said, "an' I still love 'er, poor wench."

"Why don't you go back and marry her?" asked Mary.

"An' be like me brother 'Enry?" demanded Mr. Peterkin.

"No," said Mary. "Belinda doesn't sound to me like a nagging person. I'm sure she wouldn't be like 'Enry's Maggie. And as for the twelve children, if they were your own, you'd love every one of them."

Mr. Peterkin shook his head dubiously.

Today Ann Elizabeth would not drink her milk. All she would do was to gaze enraptured at Mr. Peterkin's whiskers. Both Jean and Mary tried to make her drink, but their coaxing was in vain.

"Da-da," said Ann Elizabeth. "Pitty!"

"She thinks you're her daddy," explained Mary. "I don't know why she should, because Mr. Arlington shaved every morning. But, I guess, it's because you're tall and wear trousers. She says your whiskers are pretty. Maybe you can get her to eat."

"Me?" said Mr. Peterkin. "Well, blow me down!"

But, when he offered her the cup, she dimpled into smiles and drank every drop.

"There! You see?" cried Mary. "I guess you didn't know you had a way with babies, did you?"

" 'Ey, give 'er some more," roared Mr. Peterkin.

"Oh, I can't," said Mary. "You see, we only have that one pail of milk a week for four babies. She'll have to finish off with a banana."

"I say!" roared Mr. Peterkin. "I've three goats that give milk every day! The little beggar sha'n't starve!"

"She's not starving," said Mary, "but we *could* use some more milk. Only, you see, it's so far around the beach to your house—even if you gave us more milk, it would be pretty hard to get it oftener than once a week."

"If we had a path through the jungle, it wouldn't be so far," put in Jean eagerly.

"A path through the jungle?" repeated Mr. Peterkin.

But just then Prince Charley pulled Blue's ear, and Blue began to howl at the top of his voice. In an instant the other babies, who were sleepy and cross, joined in, and the charming dinner party ended in an uproar.

Mr. Peterkin, who had so surely seemed a reformed character, put his hands over his ears and arose in anger.

"There you go!" he cried, "abotherin' of me! You're all like peas in a pod! Meddlesome young 'uns! Meddlesome young 'uns!" And, without a "thank you" for his dinner, he clumped angrily away.

120

"Well, did you ever!" cried Mary. "Just because they cried!"

Halfred, who was enjoying himself with hardtack and singing, made no move to follow his master.

But just before the outraged seaman disappeared from sight, he turned around and shouted, "Halfred, come 'ome!"

"Oh, you would, would you?" grumbled Halfred. Then he rolled his yellow eye around at the girls as if to apologize for his master's manners. As he flew away, he sang, and the song was not "Oh, Bedelia," but "Honward, Christian Soldiers!"

CHAPTER TWELVE————————————

Several Surprises

"WELL, I guess you reformed Halfred anyway," said Jean cheerfully.

"Oh, Jeannie, what a pity!" wailed Mary. "That's the end of Mr. Peterkin, I suppose. Why couldn't the babies have put off crying?"

" 'There's nothing like a nice clean baby to hold,' " mocked Jean, who was in a particularly impish mood, after having had to sit still for so long listening to Mary's sermon.

"That naughty Charley started the whole trouble!" cried Mary. "He ought to be punished!"

But Charley was already on Jean's shoulder with his skinny arms around her neck, and he knew that he was safe.

Whether they admitted it or not, they were both much disappointed at the outcome of the party. Mr. Peterkin had seemed so much reformed, and had even been on the point of giving them more milk—perhaps even of cutting a pathway for them through the jungle. Now all was lost.

They gradually quieted the howling babies and put them down for their naps. Mary lay down also, tired from her

122

combined duties as cook, hostess, and saver of souls. Jean and Charley went up to the vine swing in the edge of the woods, and as Jean swung back and forth, back and forth, she made up one of her songs.

> *"Oh, 'e were 'aying long ago,*
> *A-'aying gay, were 'e.*
> *'E dropped a pitchfork on 'is toe,*
> *An' then 'e went to sea.*
> *Oh, Mr. Peterkin!*
> *Jolly Mr. Peterkin!*
> *Dear old Mr. Peterkin!*
> *An' then 'e went to sea-o!*
> *Oh, Mary preached a sermon fine,*
> *A sermon fine, a sermon fine,*
> *While Jean was swinging on a vine.*
> *Oh, lovely Jean! Oh, beautiful Jean!*
> *Prince Charley's fond delight-o!*
> *She really was a sight-o!*
> *'E couldn't bear a baby's cry,*
> *It nearly made the pirate 'die.*
> *'I wonder what is in his chest,*
> *Until I know I'll never rest!"*
> *Says beautiful Jean, says lovely Jean,*
> *A-swinging on her vine-o!"*

The next morning there was trouble with Jonah again.

He had appeared to be thriving on the goats' milk and had had fewer and fewer attacks of colic. He was really developing into a beautiful bouncing boy, and his outing on the desert island had given him a much better color and rounder cheeks than he had had when under the care of his fond mother. Mary was quite proud of him. But on the day after the party, he awoke screaming and screwing up his face, kicking his legs, and clawing the air with his hands.

"Whazza mazza? Whazza mazza?" begged Mary, tenderly hanging over him.

"Baby talk!" scoffed Jean. "If *his* name is Jonah, *ours* ought to be Job. We've got so many troubles. Jean Job! That would be rather nice for a change, wouldn't it? Or maybe it should be Job Jean."

"It doesn't sound like colic," murmured Mary, running through all her little tricks for appeasing crying babies. But none of them did Jonah any good. "Do you suppose he could have caught anything from Mr. Peterkin yesterday?"

"Mr. Peterkin looks healthy to me," remarked Jean. "Only the good die young."

That remark did not serve to comfort Mary at all, for naturally she considered Jonah one of the good, and the idea that *he* might be going to die young filled her with even greater alarm.

It was at this tense moment that they noticed the first

124

crashing noise from the jungle! At first it sounded like the reverberation of distant thunder, and then—*Crash!* CRASH! This was followed by more thunder and another crash.

"What is it?" gasped Mary.

For a few moments Jonah was frightened out of his howls, and the four babies looked at Mary with round questioning eyes.

"It sounds like one of those dinosaur things we had in our geography, coming through the woods and switching its tail," offered Jean.

"But the dinosaurs have all been dead these thousands of years, Jean."

"Well, I've told you my idea. Now you tell me yours."

Bang! bang! bang! *Crash!* CRASH!

"I don't know," gasped Mary. "It's horrible, isn't it?" Jonah began to howl again, and one by one the other babies joined him. Chattering wildly, Prince Charley hid his head under Jean's arm.

But at that moment a familiar face appeared. With a graceful swoop of red and green feathers, Halfred flew out of the jungle, and his horny old beak veritably seemed to smile at them.

"Man the pumps, Mary, man the pumps," croaked Halfred cheerily.

"He never called me Mary before! He's come to warn

125

us, Jean." She began to scratch his head in the place he liked and beg him to tell them of the danger.

But Halfred only winked one eye at her and remarked hoarsely, "Oh, you would, would you?"

"Mary!" cried Jean. "I know exactly what it is! It's Mr. Peterkin cutting a pathway for us through the jungle!"

"No!" said Mary, sitting down flatly on a baked banana. "But I thought we'd never see him again."

"Listen!" commanded Jean. "It's his ax that goes bang! bang! bang! and then a tree comes down *Crash!* CRASH! Halfred came ahead to tell us."

"I knew that Mr. Peterkin had a heart of gold!" cried Mary happily. "It just goes to show that you should never judge a heart by the kind of face it wears."

"But what about the babies, Mary? After all his work, it would be a pity for him to arrive here and find them all howling just the way they were when he clumped off and left them yesterday."

"Yes, it would be discouraging," admitted Mary. "I'll hand out the hardtack, and you do a highland fling for them."

Hardtack and the highland fling did wonders for the twins and Ann Elizabeth. In a moment they were smiling again, and Mary had wiped their eyes and noses. But the nearer Mr. Peterkin came with his ax, the more dismally Jonah roared.

126

"I'll have to take him down to the beach, poor suffering angel! where the sound of the waves will drown out his cries," said Mary. "You stay here, Jean, and welcome Mr. Peterkin when he comes."

Jean was glad enough to be left at the tepee, for, while she was just as fond of smiling babies as her sister, she sometimes shared Mr. Peterkin's sentiments about crying ones.

Halfred flew back and forth from the tepee to the scene of the crashing sounds, and Charley, who had lost all his fear, swung through the branches by hand, foot, and tail.

It was well after noon before Mr. Peterkin chopped his way out of the jungle. Poor Mary had not yet returned, so Jean knew that Jonah must still be crying. There was a final and most terrific crash, and then Mr. Peterkin put in his appearance. He was wet with sweat and looked more annoyed than usual.

"Well, there it is!" he said. "A path through the jungle! *I* didn't want it! It weren't *my* hidea! But there it is for them as can use it. Troublesome, I calls it."

"Oh, thank you, Mr. Peterkin!" cried Jean.

"Don't thank me," said the honest seaman crossly. "It's for me little Lizzie."

"For who?" Jean was puzzled.

"I mean 'er," said Mr. Peterkin, pointing at Ann Elizabeth. Ann Elizabeth, smiling engagingly, crawled to Mr. Peterkin's feet and stretched up her arms to be taken.

"Pitty," she said happily. "Pitty-pitty!"

"Was they trying to starve me little Lizzie?" cooed Mr. Peterkin, taking the delighted baby into his arms. "Was they tryin' to starve 'er, an' 'er old Huncle 'Arvey with all the milk she could 'old right around on t'other side of the hi'land? Bless 'er little gizzard!"

Jean stared at them as hard as she could. Then she let out a howl of delight and started to run for the beach.

"Baby talk! Mary, Mr. Peterkin's talking baby talk! Come quick!"

Mary was walking slowly up the beach with Jonah in her arms, when Jean called to her. Jonah was cooing happily, and Mary wore a rapturous smile on her tired face. But Jean saw with irritation that Mary's angelic smile had nothing whatever to do with the wonderful new path through the jungle, nor with the highly amusing fact that Mr. Peterkin was talking baby talk. She tried again.

"Mary, he's talking silly to Ann Elizabeth just the way you do! Baby talk, Mary!"

"Well, of course, that was bound to happen sooner or later, dear," said Mary. "I'm glad it's come so soon. But, oh, Jean, something most *remarkable* has happened to Jonah! *Wonderful,* Jean!"

128

Jean's mouth fell open again in surprise. If Mary could accept a path through the jungle and Mr. Peterkin's baby talk so calmly, whatever in the world had happened to Jonah to make her say "remarkable" and "wonderful"?

"Come here and look, Jeannie," she went on, "and tell me if you ever saw a more beautiful sight."

Filled with awe, Jeannie drew near and gazed into Jonah's round, pink face.

"Open up, dovey darling," begged Mary. "Open the itsy, bitsy mouthey for its ownest Mary. That's a lamb!"

Jonah gave them a wan smile, and Jean had a brief glimpse of something white showing against his red gum.

"It's just like a pearl, isn't it?" said Mary proudly.

"What?" asked Jean, still mystified.

"Why, his first tooth! Didn't you see it? That's why he was crying so this morning, poor cherub. It hurt when it was coming through. But now it's all right, and Mary's so proud of her gweat big baby boy!"

"Oh, you and Mr. Peterkin and your baby talk!" said Jean in disgust. "*I'm* going to see the trail through the jungle!" And away she went, whistling to Halfred and Charley to join her.

CHAPTER THIRTEEN

Mr. Peterkin Has His Ups and Downs

AFTER the path was cut through the jungle, Mr. Peterkin became a more and more frequent visitor at the tepee. He had decided to deliver the babies' milk himself. But the girls knew now that it was not entirely because of the milk that he came. They knew that Mr. Peterkin liked their cooking better than his own, and even more he liked to have Ann Elizabeth tell him that his beard was pretty. He insisted that Ann Elizabeth should have the freshest and richest milk, and he nearly always brought some trinket for her which he himself had carved.

Once Mr. Peterkin's hard heart had started to soften, it was just like ice cream in the sun. He began to carry the twins pickaback or ride them cockhorse on his knee, and Jonah was allowed to chew his gold watch chain. Even Mary and Jean came in for a good share of his kindliness. Naturally he still grumbled a good deal and pretended to be angry with them all, but after all one can't throw off the habits of years in a moment.

As the girls often remarked, Ann Elizabeth was probably

the cutest baby ever seen. She was plump and dimpled, with shiny curls that stood up all the wrong way on the back of her head, and big blue eyes. But it very much looked as if her fatal beauty had made her lazy. She only had to smile or point or whimper a little to have people running to bring her a drink or a banana or to lift her up and carry her about. So it had never seemed necessary to her to learn to walk. When she wanted to do a bit of exploring by herself, she went on all fours like Prince Charley.

This had begun to worry Mary. Here was Jonah with new teeth, and Ann Elizabeth still could not walk.

"Do you think possibly she's weak in the knees?" she asked Mr. Peterkin one day when he was calling.

"Not 'er! Not my Lizzie!" said that gentleman indignantly.

"She's so contented!" sighed Mary.

"Look 'ere," said Mr. Peterkin. "You need some kind of contraption for 'er. A baby walker! That's what it is."

"A baby walker?"

"That's what it is," repeated the honest seaman. "Maggie an' 'Enry 'ad one for their twelve. Bly'me, I'll make ye one!"

"It won't hurt her, will it?" asked Mary cautiously.

"Me 'urt Lizzie?" shouted Mr. Peterkin. "What do you think?"

So Mr. Peterkin constructed a beautiful baby walker out

131

of tough vines, a couple of boards, and a piece of the canvas sail. It was something like a swing, and was suspended from the branch of a tree at such a height that Ann Elizabeth's feet could easily touch the ground without having to hold up the whole weight of her own body. She pranced around delightedly, and the whole thing seemed to be a huge success.

"Well, that's some good that came out of 'Enry and Maggie anyway!" remarked Jean, as she admired Mr. Peterkin's handiwork.

But there were others who were not so pleased. Pink and Blue stood looking on, and it was more than they could bear to see Ann Elizabeth the center of all eyes.

"Ba-ba bye-bye, too!" said Blue.

"Ba-ba fwing!" added Pink.

Their lower lips began to drop lower and lower, trembling piteously. Large tears rolled silently down their cheeks. A more pathetic sight would be difficult to imagine.

"But you already know how to walk, twinsies," said Mary sensibly.

"Ba-ba go bye-bye too," persisted Blue.

"Ba-ba fwing," wept Pink.

Their lower lips continued to drop farther and farther, and suddenly they let out twin howls that echoed dismally through the jungle.

"It's no use trying to persuade them, once they make up

their minds!" said Mary. "I guess you'll just have to build two more baby walkers, Mr. Peterkin."

Mr. Peterkin behaved very nicely, indeed. With scarcely a murmur he went to work, and before the day was over the delighted twins were dangling in baby walkers too.

Jean and Prince Charley had looked on with interest all the while that Mr. Peterkin worked.

"And now," said Jean politely, when the three baby walkers were finished, "will you please make one for Charley?"

"'Ow's that?"

"A baby walker for Charley, please."

"For that monkey?"

"If you please."

"Sliver my timbers!" yelled Mr. Peterkin, "an' strike me red, white, an' blue! if you catch me making a baby walker for a monkey! No, sir! no baby walkers for no monkeys! What's 'e got 'is tail for, may I hask?"

So Charley never got his baby walker, and it must be admitted that the twins soon tired of theirs, but Ann Elizabeth's legs were greatly strengthened and benefited by hers. One day she was sitting on the tarpaulin outside of the tepee when she saw Mr. Peterkin coming through the jungle with his milk, and, rising on unsteady legs, she took her very first steps to meet him. Mr. Peterkin thought that that was the smartest thing a baby had ever been known to do. After a while even Mary got a little tired of hearing Mr. Peterkin tell about it.

"Of course all babies learn to walk *sometime*," she said sensibly. "I suppose you did the same thing yourself when you were a baby, or you'd still be going around on fours."

"But look 'ere!" cried Mr. Peterkin. "The little beggar walked to *me*, she did. It weren't just a hordinary first step. She got right up an' came awalkin' to *me*, an' 'Pitty!' she says, areachin' for my chin, 'Pitty!' "

Jean had had some hopes of finding out what was in Mr.

Peterkin's chest, now that he had grown so tender hearted. On one of her cleaning days she baked Mr. Peterkin a beautiful pie full of sliced bananas and pieces of cocoanut whipped up with gulls' eggs and sugar. It seemed like a wonderful mixture to Jean, and all it needed was a bit of flavoring, but unfortunately she couldn't find either vanilla or nutmeg in Mr. Peterkin's cupboard. However, there was plenty of garlic, and, knowing that this was the honest seaman's favorite flavor, Jean put it in with a lavish hand.

The pie came out of the oven a beautiful, golden brown, and, when Jean set it before Mr. Peterkin at luncheon, she felt that this was the very moment to ask him about his chest.

"Hah!" said Mr. Peterkin, rubbing his hands together with delight, and preparing to plunge his knife into the pie. "Blow me down, if it ain't a tart, an' w'at a tart at that!"

"Mr. Peterkin," said Jean hurriedly, "sometime will you let me see what's in your chest? Really I think I ought to clean it out for you. You know moths might get in or rust corrupt. May I?"

"Well, now, little Jeannie—" began Mr. Peterkin amiably, raising the first forkful of pie to his lips.

"Yes—yes?" said Jeannie eagerly.

But, at the first taste of pie, Mr. Peterkin's eyes suddenly seemed to start from his head. He gave a loud, strangling cough and started for the door. This was a very bad omen,

135

indeed. Jean sniffed at the pie and it did smell strongly of garlic, but after all if garlic was Mr. Peterkin's favorite flavor—

"No!" roared Mr. Peterkin. "Don't you *never* look in that chest no 'ow! Do you 'ear? An' mind you've fed that tart to the goats an' gulls before I get back."

Away went Mr. Peterkin to the jungle. Only one thing was clear to Jean. There was something about the combination of bananas, cocoanut, sugar, and garlic that brought out the worst in a reformed man. That was the second "No!" she'd had out of Mr. Peterkin, and it proved to Jean that the battle wasn't entirely won yet. She looked wistfully at the brass-bound chest and wondered if it were lost forever.

It was about this time that Mary consulted her calendar one day and saw that Christmas was approaching.

"We haven't any place to hang our stockings," said Jean.

"Oh, we can fix up something. We must have a real Christmas for the babies' sakes. It would be awful if they grew up without knowing about Christmas."

"And we can make presents for them too! And, Mary, let's give Mr. Peterkin and Halfred presents!"

"Why, of course!" said Mary. "What did you think?"

After that the tepee buzzed with mystery and excitement. The girls were busy making presents out of clam and

136

cocoanut shells, palm leaves, moss, clay, and sticks, anything they could find which gave them an idea for a gift.

"W'at's this? W'at's this?" inquired Mr. Peterkin, arriving one day with his milk while they were in the midst of their preparations.

"Oh, Mr. Peterkin, it's for Christmas!" said Mary, and Jean sang:

> *"We live on an island*
> *And not on an isthmus,*
> *But we can have Christmas*
> *And Christmas and Christmas!"*

"*Christmas!*" said Mr. Peterkin. "Blow me down! I'd forgotten there was such!" He kept saying over and over "*Christmas!* Strike me pink!" and before he left that day, he had invited them all to his house to hang up their stockings over his stove and to eat Christmas dinner from his table!

"But no garlic in the pudding!" he warned.

Jean blushed, but naturally Mary paid no attention to such a silly remark.

"I'm so glad," she said. "I want the babies to get used to things as they are at home—and Christmas in a tent *is* rather odd! Thank you, Mr. Peterkin."

"Don't mention it, Miss," said Mr. Peterkin, and Jean added sensibly, "Christmas is nice anywhere, Mary."

137

CHAPTER FOURTEEN

Lost in the Storm

THE day before Christmas Mr. Peterkin invited Mary over to bake and opened his precious larder to her. On his shelves he had a barrel of flour, a small keg of molasses, a tin of raisins, and ever so many things that could be turned into Christmas by a clever girl like Mary. Mr. Peterkin himself declared that he was going out to shoot a fowl for roasting.

"But mind, no garlic!" he warned.

"Whatever does he mean?" thought Mary. "It must be some kind of joke."

As Mary hurried along the jungle path to Mr. Peterkin's, she wondered if she should leave Jean all alone with the babies today. There was such a queer look in the sky. The sweet, fair blue was hidden by sulphur-colored clouds which cast a sinister glare over the familiar landscape. But Mary knew that the babies were safe in their pen, and that Jean was busy finishing a beautiful cocoanut ashtray for Mr. Peterkin—and, of course, there was no cause to worry about them.

138

She took possession of the shanty with such a bustle of rattling pans, sifting of flour, and boiling of kettles that Halfred could scarcely find a corner in which to perch in peace.

Mary was all excited because she had decided to undertake the making of a bag pudding. She had often helped Aunt Emma to make such a Christmas treat, and knew just how to flour the cloth, pour in the pudding, tie it all up in a great ball, and drop it into boiling water. But to do it all alone was something which required not only skill but courage. Mary had both, and so she went busily to work.

"Of course, pudding won't do for the babies," she said to herself, "but I'll make a nice custard for them out of gulls' eggs and goats' milk. It will be much more suitable."

As the day went on, the sky grew darker and darker, and Mary sometimes paused in her preparations to look anxiously out of the shanty window. She had just set the custards aside to cool and was cautiously turning the pudding in the boiling water, when the weather was again brought to her attention by a great clap of thunder that seemed to rock the island. This was followed by such a blast of wind and rain that Mary thought for a moment the shanty would be swept away.

She quickly put the pudding pot on the back of the stove so that it would not boil over, caught up an old sou'wester and slicker of Mr. Peterkin's, and hurried out into the storm. It was almost as dark as night outside, and the rain came down in torrents. It was the only bad storm they had had, and Mary's first thought was for the babies. Would the tepee weather this wind and rain? How could Jean handle all the babies alone?

"Oh, my children! My children!" cried Mary, as she hurried along. About halfway through the jungle, she met Mr. Peterkin. With his gun and two plump wild fowl still slung over his shoulder, he came crashing through the underbrush.

"W'ere's my Lizzie?" he cried wildly.

"At the tepee," shouted Mary. "Run!"

They ran, and, above the crashing of the storm and the rattling of palm leaves, they could hear the roar of the waterfall that came down near the tepee. Its usual pleasant gurgle had grown suddenly loud and menacing. As they came in sight of the tepee, they saw that the stream had already risen high enough to reach the tepee door, and was whirling away some of their shell and cocoanut dishes.

"Jean!" called Mary. "Jean! Jean!"

A pitiful crying was her only answer, and, running to the pen, she found Ann Elizabeth and Pink, dripping wet, clinging to the sides of it. But Jean, Jonah, Blue, and Prince Charley were nowhere to be found!

Mr. Peterkin grabbed the two babies up under his arms, and just in time, too, for the water was already rising inside the pen. Then he and Mary saved what they could of the furnishings of the tepee and took them to higher ground, before the rising torrent swept the tepee away.

"*Oh!*" cried Mary. "*Oh! Oh!*" It was all she could think of to say, as she stood with white face and clasped hands, watching the mass of canvas and bamboo, which had been the tepee, rushing away to the sea.

"I say! You'll get your feet wet, Mary," roared Mr. Peterkin, pulling Mary back from the rising stream.

"*Jean! Jean!*" called Mary. But her voice was lost in the noise of storm and stream and lashing trees.

They searched frantically for some time, but not a trace of the missing four could be found.

"Oh, I don't know what to do!" cried Mary in despair.

"Now, lookee 'ere," shouted Mr. Peterkin, "you an' them babies is agoin' to catch pneumony like that. You go to my shanty and get warm an' dry an' put them babies to bed in my bed, and I'll go lookin' for the others!"

It seemed the best thing to do, and so Mary obeyed. When Pink and Ann Elizabeth were warm, dry, and asleep in Mr. Peterkin's bed, she put on the sou'wester again.

"Halfred," she said to the parrot, "I've got to go and look for my Jean. You mind the babies now, will you?"

141

"Well, bless my soul and body!" said Halfred in surprise. But he moved from his perch on the phonograph, and took up a watchful position on the back of a chair near the bed.

"Good Halfred!" said Mary. "It's a hard time for all of us!" And out she went again into the storm, calling: "Jean! Jean! Where are you? Where are you?" The wind still took her little voice and tossed it like nothing into the great sound of the storm. Rain and tears were all mixed on her pale cheeks. When she had gone a little way into the jungle, Mary met Mr. Peterkin coming back. He shook his head.

" 'Tis no use," he said. "They're surely gone!"

"Oh, no!" said Mary. "I won't give up yet!" Back into the jungle they went. Rain blinded them, mud slipped under their feet, vines tripped and tangled them, but still Mary pushed on, searching and calling.

Gradually the sky began to grow lighter, and the storm to abate. What a scene of desolation it was! Trees broken or torn up by their roots, streams swollen and muddy, plants broken and crushed by the deluge.

"Oh, what is to become of us?" cried Mary. "Jean and two babies lost! The tepee swept away! The lovely island spoiled!"

"Don't you fret," said Mr. Peterkin, "long as I've a 'ome, 'tis yours."

"But you don't like children," sobbed Mary.

"Whoever said that?" cried Mr. Peterkin angrily. "I'm huncommon fond o' young 'uns, I am!"

Suddenly there was a chattering in the trees above them, and a little brown animal swung himself down to Mary's shoulder and put skinny arms around her neck.

"*Charley!*" cried Mary. "Oh, Charley, you beautiful, blessed monkey! Where are Jean and the babies?"

As if he understood, Charley jumped from Mary's shoulder and began to go ahead of them through the woods. It was difficult to follow him, because, whenever Charley came to a fallen tree or a dense thicket, he jumped into the branches overhead and swung along with his hands and tail. But, scratched and torn and sorely discouraged, somehow or other Mary and Mr. Peterkin managed to follow him. Mary half suspected that the mischievous fellow was leading them a wild-goose chase, and yet they had no choice but to follow him. At last, chattering noisily, he disappeared under a ledge of rock that formed a sort of cave or shelter.

" 'E's 'aving 'is fun with us," said Mr. Peterkin gloomily, but Mary stooped down and looked under the ledge. And there sat Jean and Jonah and Blue! Jean screamed.

"Don't yell, Jeannie," soothed Mary. "We've found you!"

"Oh, Mary!" cried Jean, jumping up and bumping her head on the ledge. "I've never been so lost and wet in my life. It was awful! I never thought I'd live to tell the tale! But did you rescue Ann Elizabeth and Pink?"

"Yes! Yes!" cried Mary. "Oh, Jean, I'm so thankful we found you! *How* did it happen?"

"Oh, Mary, Blue climbed out of the pen. You know what a climber he is, and I am sure that Charley helped him. I just caught a glimpse of them as they were disappearing into the jungle. I couldn't leave Jonah, so I just grabbed him up and ran after them. And they were very naughty and kept me chasing them a long time, and then the storm came and we were lost. We went around and around, and couldn't get out, and finally we found that ledge to sit under."

"Well, I just hope you weren't as scared as I was," cried Mary.

"*Scared?*" shouted Jean. "Nobody's ever been scareder in this world! Oh, Mary, I'm so tired of this old island! I want to go home where Father is!" Jean burst out crying, and there were tears in Mary's eyes, too, as she repeated, "Home?"

"Oh, yes!" cried Jeannie passionately. "Of course it's a nice island, and it's better than the bottom of the sea—but, oh! I want Father or Aunt Emma and streets and automobiles and places where you don't get lost in the jungle when it storms!"

"Jean," said Mary gravely, "we haven't sung 'Scots, Wha' Hae' for a long time. We're—we're kind of losing our grip."

144

"Maybe—we—are," gulped Jean.

There was a moment's pause while Jean stifled her sobs in a very wet blue handkerchief. Then with a quavering voice she joined Mary's clear treble:

> *"By oppression's woes an' pains,*
> *By your sons in servile chains,*
> *We will drain our dearest veins,*
> *But they shall be free.*
> *Lay the proud usurpers low!*
> *Tyrants fall in every foe!*
> *Liberty's in every blow!*
> *Let us do or dee!"*

Mr. Peterkin looked at them in amazement, for some magic in the old battle song of the descendants of William Wallace always put new heart into Mary and Jean, and now they dried their tears like Scottish heroes.

"Well, blow me down!" exclaimed Mr. Peterkin.

"Oh, please don't say 'Blow me down,'" begged Jean, with chattering teeth. "I've had enough wind for one day! Let's go to the tepee."

"The tepee's gone," said Mary.

"Gone?" echoed Jean. "But where can we live?"

"Come! Come!" said Mr. Peterkin gruffly. "The shanty's your 'ome, an' 'igh time it were ye was in it, adryin' of yourselves! Give me them babies, an' move along now!"

145

CHAPTER FIFTEEN

The Chest

A**S THEY** sat about Mr. Peterkin's stove that evening, Mary suddenly remembered.

"It's Christmas eve, you know," she said.

"Oh, Mary, did all our presents get washed away with the tepee?" asked Jean.

"I'm afraid so. We'll have to make the best of it."

"You 'ang up your stockings just the same," said Mr. Peterkin mysteriously.

He was dandling Ann Elizabeth and Jonah on his knees, while the twins were pretending to be wild animals snapping about his ankles. Drying clothes steamed all about him, and, if ever anyone saw a more contented picture of a family man, I should be very much surprised.

"Do you have 'Silent Night' or any Christmas records for your phonograph?" asked Mary.

"I've got 'Jingle Bells,' " said Mr. Peterkin.

"Oh, let me play it," begged Jean.

So the phonograph was wound up, and everyone joined Halfred in singing the jolly old song.

It brought back to Mary all the gay, snowy Christmases that she had known in the United States. How odd to be here on a desert island for Christmas! Jean's remark that she was tired of Baby Island echoed sadly in Mary's heart. It was fun for a while, but after all Father and home were best. Would they ever see them again? Resolutely Mary put these thoughts out of her mind.

Before the babies were put to bed, the girls and Mr. Peterkin hung their tiny stockings on the shelf behind the stove. The poor little socks were worn and old now, but Mary had kept them clean and well darned for just such an occasion as this. Although the babies could scarcely have been expected to understand it, Mary told them the sweet, familiar Christmas story, and even Halfred and Charley listened respectfully. Then the four babies were tucked in a comfortable row in Mr. Peterkin's bed. It had been agreed that Mary and Jean would roll up in blankets on the floor, and Mr. Peterkin insisted that he would sleep in his hammock under the palm trees.

"It seems too bad to drive Mr. Peterkin out of his own house, and for a lot of 'meddlesome young 'uns' too!" said Jean.

"I know," said Mary. "Tomorrow we'll have to start building a new house." But there was no enthusiasm in her voice. It seemed to her that they had been on Baby Island a very long time, and it was hard to have to begin again.

Perhaps the reformed seaman sensed the feeling of gloom which had fixed itself on the girls this Christmas eve, for suddenly he said: "Well, well, it's been a 'ard day, an' Miss Jean 'ere 'as 'ad a 'ard time. I been thinkin' I'd like to do something for 'er to cheer 'er up, sort of."

"For me?" said Jean, all in a flutter.

"There's something I do once a year, that might be of interest to 'er."

"Something you do?"

"Aye, can you guess what?"

"You—you play the phonograph."

"No, something more hunusual."

148

"You dust off *Pharaoh's Horses.*"

"I 'ates dusting."

"Then you—you count your clamshells."

"No."

Jean was wriggling with excitement, because all the time she had been thinking of something which she hadn't dared suggest. Now she came out with it.

"*You open your chest!*"

"Aye, that I do," said Mr. Peterkin calmly.

> *"Oh, chest! chest!*
> *Beautiful chest!"*

sang Jean, hopping up and down on one foot.

> *"Oh, what is inside*
> *The chest so wide?*
> *Oh, beautiful, bee-autiful chest!"*

"Hush! hush! You'll wake the babies!" cautioned Mary.

Mr. Peterkin took a clumsy key out of his pocket.

"I made this 'ere myself. There weren't no key to this lock when first I 'appened onto the chest."

"You found it on the island?" asked Jean breathlessly.

"That I did," said Mr. Peterkin. "'Alf buried in sand it were, just up in the cove where 'igh tide couldn't reach it."

"Were it a pirate chest?" asked Jean, so excited that she had unconsciously fallen into Mr. Peterkin's manner of speech.

"I think it were, lass," said Mr. Peterkin solemnly.

"You aren't making this up, are you, Mr. Peterkin?" asked Mary doubtfully.

"No, ma'am!" replied the honest seaman, flushing proudly. "This 'ere is the one hadventure that ever really 'appened to me. This one weren't drab. It weren't tame. This one really 'appened to me."

"Was there anything in the chest?" asked Jean in a hoarse whisper.

"You take this 'ere key an' look," said Mr. Peterkin, putting the key in Jean's hand. " 'Tis just the way I found it."

Jean inserted the key in the massive lock and was about to turn it when she remembered her conversation with Mary.

"There aren't any dead ladies—or—or diseases—or—or skellingtons in it, are there?"

"No—no—no!"

"Poltroons?"

"I don't know what poltroons is."

"She means doubloons," put in Mary. "Poltroons are cowards, but Jean always gets them mixed up with the word for Spanish money."

"Well, strike me pink!" said Mr. Peterkin. "You been tryin' to get at that chest ever since you come 'ere, and now when I give ye the key, you stand there like a zany an' hask me what's in it!"

Suddenly Jean left the chest, flung her arms around Mr. Peterkin's neck, and kissed him on the end of the nose. While he was still gasping like a stranded fish, she flew back to the chest, turned the lock, and flung open the cover. And, sure enough, *it was full of Spanish gold!* Old, old pieces, dull with time and weather, but still they were gold!

Mary was the first to speak.

"Well, I never saw so much money in my life," she said. "There's enough there to put the babies through college!"

"What are you going to do with it?" asked Jean breathlessly.

"I don't rightly know," said Mr. Peterkin calmly. "There isn't much need for money on a desert hi'land. I thought some day to get Belinda a silk dress—"

"That would be nice," said Jean. "Does she have brown hair? You might get her a red silk one and a little black hat with a red feather."

"But I've more than I want," said Mr. Peterkin, "an' 'tis Christmas eve. Fetch me the sugar scoop." Wondering what the sugar scoop had to do with pirate gold, Jean obeyed. Mr. Peterkin filled the scoop with golden pieces, and then with great solemnity he began to fill the babies' stockings. A scoopful of gold for every stocking!

Mary and Jean watched him in awed silence. What a

151

curious Santa Claus! And wasn't he pouring a small fortune into the babies' socks?

"Where's yours?" demanded Mr. Peterkin, when he had finished with the babies'.

"But ours are so big," protested Mary politely.

" 'Ang them up," said Mr. Peterkin. "Ye deserve all ye get."

So Mary and Jean watched him fill each of their stockings with gold until they were so heavy that they seemed in danger of bursting.

"Think what that will buy us," said Mary, "*if* we ever get off the island!"

Long after she was supposed to be sound asleep, Jean kept opening an eye to look at her heavy stocking, hanging above the stove and faintly lighted by the last glow of the coals.

"*If* I ever get back," she thought to herself, "I'll get me another silk dress like the one the baby whale is wearing *and* a new doll like Miranda. But best of all was the fun of unlocking the chest and getting the first peep inside!"

CHAPTER SIXTEEN

An Answer to Jean's Letters

AFTER the storm, Christmas day dawned clear and bright. As soon as she was awake, Jean rubbed her eyes and looked at the row of stockings. They were still there, sagging with gold, so the mysterious chest was not a dream.

Mr. Peterkin brought in a little tropical tree which looked a good deal like a northern Christmas tree, and they trimmed it with more of the pirate gold. Fastened on the branches with string and tree gum, the quaint old golden pieces made a very pretty decoration. After the tree was trimmed, and they had dressed the babies and eaten breakfast and milked the goats, Mr. Peterkin, with his whiskers floured to look like Santa Claus, handed out the gifts.

Besides the stockings full of gold, which Mr. Peterkin seemed to consider of scarcely any consequence, he brought in a number of mysterious objects of which he was evidently very proud. It appeared that while the girls had been spending hours on the presents which were all swept away with the tepee, the good old seaman had not been idle. He had made a little bamboo chair for his "Lizzie," and a

153

hardwood teething ring for Jonah, on which Jonah immediately celebrated by cutting his second tooth. For the twins he had made rattles by wiring together a couple of shells with tiny pebbles inclosed between them, and a neat handle of the bent wire. As a delicate final touch, Elisha's shells were pink, and Elijah's a pale blue. For Mary and Jean, Mr. Peterkin had carved two baskets out of cocoanut shells, highly polished, with their names carefully engraved upon the sides.

"But these are *beautiful!*" cried Mary.

"Better than gold?" asked Mr. Peterkin hopefully.

"Better than gold," said Mary, "because you made them your very own self."

Even Halfred and Charley had gifts—large pieces of hardtack, decorated with red berries and green leaves.

"Well, what's to stop us 'aving our dinner?" inquired Mr. Peterkin, when the gifts had been distributed, and this time Mary did not make him listen to a sermon. Indeed, he did not seem in need of quite so many texts today.

The girls bustled about the stove and larder, and presently such a meal was served up as Mr. Peterkin's shanty had never known before. Roast wild fowl, hot biscuits, baked breadfruit, bamboo shoots for salad, with a grand climax of plum pudding for the elders and custard for the babies.

154

As the plum pudding, steaming hot, and wreathed in laurel leaves, was borne to the table, Mr. Peterkin started the phonograph to playing "In the Shade of the Old Apple Tree." Halfred commenced to sing, Charley to dance, and the babies to bounce themselves up and down in their chairs and to beat on the table with their spoons. Jean and Mary joined in the fun with shouts of laughter, and Mr. Peterkin suddenly began to do a sailor's hornpipe. They were all making so much racket that they didn't hear a very unusual noise which sounded far out in the bay. It sounded again, and still they didn't hear it. It was only when everyone fell silent to watch Mary cut the pudding that they heard it— the hoarse blast of a steamer whistle!

Mary dropped the knife to the table with a clatter, and everyone paused just where he was, listening. It sounded once again, nearer and clearer.

"Oh!" cried Mary. "A *boat!*"

"A boat!" cried Jean. "A boat! a boat!" and even Mr. Peterkin exclaimed, "A boat!"

Snatching up the babies, they all tumbled out of the shanty and ran down to shore. Halfred, following on the wing, was the only one who could think of anything to say.

"Well, bless my soul and body!" said Halfred.

She was not a large boat—more like a private yacht than a commercial steamer. She came in as far as she could and dropped anchor. The eager watchers on the shore saw a small boat lowered, manned, and rowed swiftly toward them. In it were five men, two in sailor costume, the others evidently landsmen.

"Who can they be?" wondered Mary.

"Maybe it's the pirates coming for their chest," said Jean.

"They mean us no good," said Mr. Peterkin suspiciously, running back to the shanty for his gun and his binoculars. But, when he returned a moment later, the small boat had landed, and he was just in time to see a most peculiar sight. The two sailors were busy pulling up the boat, but their three passengers had sprung on shore and were behaving like crazy men. One of these strange gentlemen had seized Mr. Peterkin's "Lizzie" and was covering her with kisses, another gentleman was completely occupied with the three Snodgrass babies, and Mary and Jean clung wildly to the third gentleman, crying, "Father! Father! Father!"

The only thing Mr. Peterkin could possibly think of to say was, "Blow me down!"

"Oh, Father," cried Mary, "however did you find us? And we thought that Mr. Arlington and Mr. Snodgrass were drowned with the *Orminta!* How *did* you all get here?"

"You see, the *Orminta* didn't sink after all," said Mr. Wallace. "Another vessel arrived and took the passengers off after your lifeboat had floated away. Your boat was cast off by mistake."

"By mistake?" repeated Mary, in a daze.

"In the first alarm people thought that the steamer would sink before help could reach her, and in the confusion your boat was cast adrift too soon. But that is all long past. The great miracle is that we have found you!"

"But how *did* you know where to find us, Father?" cried Mary.

"It was difficult," said her father. "We have been cruising around in these waters for some time now. Mr. Arlington hired the yacht and took us all with him. But we knew that you were alive and well and somewhere near."

"How did you know that, Daddy?"

"Why, because of Jean's letters to Aunt Emma, of course."

"*Jean's letters to Aunt Emma?*"

"Yes, indeed. They were picked up here and there, always in these waters. One of them was mailed to Aunt Emma, and two or three others were reported to the government, or to the shipping companies, and we were able to get hold of them. We never could have found you without them."

"Dear me!" said Jean, as surprised as anybody. "I *am* a smart girl after all, aren't I?"

On board the yacht were Mrs. Snodgrass, Mrs. Arlington, and the poodle, and the family reunions that day were

157

beautiful. Mr. Peterkin looked on with ever-softening heart.

"Touching, I calls it," he murmured to himself. "Touching, if you hask me!"

There were so many places of interest on the island to show the parents that it was decided not to leave until the next day. They must see the site of the tepee, the path through the jungle, the Christmas tree, and have a taste of Mary's pudding. But, when they entered the shanty, they were amazed to see that the pudding had almost entirely vanished. On either side of the table sat Charley and Halfred with fat stomachs and drowsy eyes. Their guilty looks betrayed them.

"Never mind!" cried Mrs. Arlington. "There's lots of food on board the yacht, and some day Mary shall make us another pudding."

"And there weren't no garlic in it neither!" lamented Mr. Peterkin.

That night the children spent on board the anchored yacht, and the next morning they went ashore again for a few last belongings and to say farewell to Mr. Peterkin and Halfred, of whom they had grown so very fond.

"Oh, Mary," said Jean. "It's nice to be going home and all, and it's just what I wanted to happen and too good to be true and everything else, but, oh dear! I do hate to go away and leave Mr. Peterkin and Halfred!"

"I know," said Mary. "It's been on my mind, too! Who'll

158

do their cooking and their cleaning? And they've got so used to babies now, I think they'll miss us!"

But Mr. Peterkin had been planning his own future. As they came ashore they saw Mr. Peterkin locking his shanty. Halfred was on his shoulder, looking rather pale about the eyes and beak from too much Christmas pudding. In Mr. Peterkin's hand was his dufflebag, out of which protruded the purple morning-glory horn of his precious phonograph, and beside him on the beach lay his chest of gold.

"Give me a 'and with this chest, will ye, mates?" he called to the sailors, and to the girls he said: "I couldn't bear to stay. Baby Hi'land without no babies! 'Twould be too lonesome now. I'm agoin' 'ome an' marry my Belinda, I am!"

"Oh, Mr. Peterkin! I'm glad you've seen the light!" cried Mary, and, to Mr. Peterkin's great embarrassment, Jean repeated what she had done on Christmas eve. She threw her arms around Mr. Peterkin's neck and kissed him on the nose.

"And after you are married," said Mary, "why don't you come to Australia and live near us?"

"I been athinkin' of that," said Mr. Peterkin, "if your Pappy wouldn't mind, and would help me to locate some land."

"I shall be delighted!" cried Mr. Wallace, cordially shaking the honest seaman's hand.

"And you'll bring Halfred, won't you?" begged the girls.

159

BABY ISLAND

"Aye, Halfred and me is mates, ain't we, Halfred? I'll not be leavin' 'im!"

While they had so much desired it, there was yet something a little sad about leaving Baby Island. Living there had been a great adventure!

"We were very happy," said Mary, "even if it was hard."

"Yes," agreed Jean. "It was a real nice place to stop over at on our way to Australia."

They went to the stern of the yacht as she steamed away, and watched Baby Island as long as they could see it on the blue horizon. The babies were busy with their mothers, who could not get enough of them after such a long separation, so that Mary and Jean stood alone.

They waved their handkerchiefs to the empty island until it was out of sight.

"Well," said Mary, "it was better than borrowing babies for an afternoon anyway. Just think, we had them for nearly three months. Jonah got his first tooth, Ann Elizabeth learned to walk, and the twins to talk. It was better than never having had babies."

"Yes," said Jean. "It was worth all we went through. Of course, there are sure to be babies in Australia that we can borrow, and anyway, Mary, we have *one* of our babies left."

Prince Charley, who had been swinging in the rigging by his tail, leaped down to her shoulder and put his skinny little arms about her neck.

160